LEE DORSEY

The Hero of New France
A Call to War at Long Sault

First published by Editions Dedicaces in 2018

Copyright © Lee Dorsey, 2018

ISBN: 978-1-77076-698-3

This book was professionally typeset on Reedsy.
Find out more at reedsy.com

DEDICATION

To two of my boyhood friends
Thomas F. Buser & Wayne D. McNair

ACKNOWLEDGEMENT

Frances Parkman 1823-1893
To the man who enlightened me to the early history of North America
And translated the Jesuit Relations into the English language

Dollard des Ormeaux (called Daulac on his death certificate) was the garrison commander of the fort of Ville-Marie (Montreal) in 1660. Nothing is known of Dollard's activities prior to his arrival in Canada in 1658, except that he had a military career in France. What motivated him to come to the New World remains a mystery.

The reason given for Adam Daulac (Adam Dollard) and his companions for ambushing the Iroquois is up for debate. Tradition holds that Dollard anticipated an Iroquois attack on Ville-Marie (Montreal). In response, he amassed a small force of seventeen Frenchmen, four Algonquians, and about forty Huron's. They fought to the death and saved the Ville-Marie from invasion.

For over a century Dollard des Ormeaux became a figure in Montreal and Quebec, as he exemplified selfless personal sacrifice, as well as martyrdom for the church and for the colony.

One

*I*n the year 1635, a second son was born to an aristocratic family in the city of Ormeaux, Brie, France. He was christened Adam Daulac, Sieur des Ormeaux. His father was a Duke and a member of the Court of Louis XIV, the Sun King.

Adam had every advantage of a child that was born into a 17th century French aristocracy. At five years of age, he was enrolled into the best elementary school in Ormeaux, Brie.

Adam was a bright child, and his intellect was obvious from the beginning. Nothing but the highest grades would satisfy his demanding father, and after six years of elementary education he was enrolled into the French Military Academy at Coetquidan. The school specialized in training officers in the Infantry and Cavalry. The average student graduated around the age of nineteen and was commissioned as a lieutenant in the army.

On June 1, 1654, Adam graduated with honors and was commissioned an officer in the French army. He was assigned to command a platoon of soldiers who were responsible to guard the King when he was in Paris.

Adam took an apartment along the Left Bank, and he was invited to attend many inspiring hosts' gatherings in and about the city. He made many friends and was introduced to young ladies of means who were looking for a romantic liaison. One such seventeen-year-old beauty was Geruese Jovet. Her father was one of most wealthy and connected men in Paris in 1654. He held his daughter in the highest of esteem.

When Geruese's father was introduced to Adam, he immediately saw passion in the young man's eyes, and he instinctively knew that he had to carefully watch his daughter while she was in the company of Monsieur Daulac.

Adam was allowed to call on Geruese at her home, but he was forbidden to make contact with her on the outside, or at any of the salons where many young people socialized in the 1650s.

As with many of the young people in their late teens and early twenties, Adam and Geruese were completely obsessed with one another and their hormones were raging. One evening, while visiting Geruese at her home and surrounded by her mother and aunt, Adam managed to slip her a note. The note instructed her to meet him three days hence at noon in a coffee house of which they were both familiar.

The day before the intended meeting, Adam learned that the King was coming to Paris that same day as his preplanned meeting with Geruese, and he was ordered to have his platoon in place to meet him. He hurriedly drafted a letter to Geruese and took it to the Lycee Louis-le-Grand school, where he saw Marguerite, Geruese's best friend, entering the building. She promised Adam that she would deliver the letter to Geruese during their class on etiquette.

Good to her word, Marguerite entered the class first. When Geruese arrived and took her assigned seat, Marguerite passed the letter via another young woman to Geruese. The quick eyes of Sister Catherine saw the exchange, and she took possession of the letter before Geruese could open and read its contents.

Sister Catherine, at the end of the class, took the letter to the

Mother Superior. In turn, the Mother Superior had a Novitiate hand deliver the letter to Geruese's father. When he read its contents he became infuriated. He considered Adam's conduct as disrespectful toward his daughter and toward him as well. Adam was no longer welcome to come to his house and court Geruese.

When Geruese learned that the King was coming to Paris, she was aware that Adam would have been called to duty and would not have been able to a liaison that previous Wednesday. Geruese managed to get a letter to Adam through Marguerite who had considerable more freedom to move about than she. Once Adam read Geruese's letter and learned that his communication had been intercepted, he had every intention of approaching Geruese's father to make an offer of apology for his poor conduct and beg for his forgiveness.

However, he was engaged with his duties as the Platoon Leader and guarding the King. Originally, the King was to stay in Paris for two weeks before returning to Versailles. The King learned that an invasion from England was being planned, so he entered into defensive plans with his generals.

The two-week stay of the King extended into several weeks and eventually two months. All this time, Adam was confined to the base and was unable to leave for any reason. About the time the King was planning to leave Paris, Adam received word that his father had been taken ill and it was feared that he may die. Adam depended on the stipend he received every month from his father's estate. If his father were to die, Adam, being the second son, would not be the primogeniture of his estate, and would be left with only the money he received from his military duties. This situation could impair any plans he had to request the hand of Geruese in marriage.

As soon as the King left for Versailles, Adam left for Ormeaux Brie to be with his father on his death bed. When he arrived, he was ushered into his father's bedroom and sat by his side.

His brother had been there for several days and was making plans to take over the family's estate. Adam and his brother were several years apart and had never bonded due to their age difference.

As Adam sat by his father's bed, his brother entered the room. Adam turned to his brother Hamnet and said, "Brother, how have you been? It's been two years since I last saw you."

"How are things in Paris? It's been a long time since I was last there," Hamnet inquired.

Ignoring his question, Adam asked, "How long has father been in this state?"

"The doctor said he has had a stroke. He's chances of recovery are slim to none," Hamnet responded.

"I will sit with him through part of the night if you're agreeable. However, I haven't had a chance to see Pauline since I arrived. I would like to spend a few minutes with her." Adam stood from the side of the bed.

"Pauline is in the other room. I suggested that she leave father's side, since she was uncontrollably crying. The noise was disturbing him."

Adam stood for a moment looking down at his father and then he turned and walked slowly into the other room. Sitting in a chair sobbing, Pauline, with rosary in hand, was silently praying. When she saw Adam enter the room, she stood as he took her into his arms. Pauline was a young woman, sixteen years of age, and was always very close to Adam through their formative years.

After a few minutes of a consoling embrace, Pauline asked, "If father dies, is it possible for you to remain here with me?"

4

Adam took a long pause before he said, "There's nothing more I would like to do, however, you have to remember that I am in the army and I have my duty to King and country. Hamnet will be here with you and he will take father's place as head of the family."

At that moment, Hamnet walked into the room. "Father's breathing has become labored. I don't expect him to last the night." After a slight pause, Hamnet said, "Before father lapsed into his coma-like state, he instructed me to give you ten thousand livres as your inheritance, and then told me to encourage you to go to New France and fight for our King and country."

Adam responded by saying, "I'm not sure that I want to leave France at this time. I've met a young woman with whom I would like to spend my life, that is, if she will have me and her father will permit it." The three of them sat looking at one another without saying anything more.

After sitting with his father for a few hours, Adam spent the rest of the night in his old boyhood room.

Noise from the servants walking around outside his room in the morning awakened him. He got out of bed and with water in a small pan on the night table splashed some in his face. A knock was heard at his door.

When he opened the door, his brother announced that their father had passed away in the middle of the night. An undertaker had been called and a funeral was planned two days hence. A messenger was sent to Versailles to inform the King that their father had succumbed.

Adam excused himself and continued to get dressed. He wanted to go to Pauline and comfort her.

The next few days passed slowly, but it gave him time to think about how he was going to approach Geruese's father to ask for her hand in marriage.

After the funeral, and as Adam was packing his bag to leave, Hamnet came to his room and gave him the ten thousand livres that their father had instructed. Before he left the family home, he sat quietly with his sister Pauline. He assured her that eventually some young man would come into her life and her future years would be filled with happiness.

As he left the house that day, he was resigned that it would be for the last time.

When he arrived back in Paris, his first stop was at the barracks of his platoon. He spoke with his commanding officer and requested a few more days of leave to attend to some personal business.

That evening, he went to the coffee shop where he knew that Marguerite frequented. As he entered the shop, he took a table in the back where he could see who was coming and going.

A half hour later, Marguerite and a few of her classmates came through the door. Geruese was not among them. He raised his arm and waved toward Marguerite to motion for her to come over to his table. Marguerite was a very attractive young woman, and as she walked the length of the shop she drew a lot of male attention.

Adam invited her to join him. She sat down in a chair close to him. Adam began by asking, "How have you been?"

"Other than Nicolas beginning his studies to become a Jesuit, I've been just fine," she said sarcastically.

"I always knew that Nicolas had the calling." Adam took a slight pause. "However, you are a beautiful young woman and another young man will eventually seek you out," he assured her.

"If you called me over to ask about Geruese, you're wasting

your time. Her father brings her to school each day and is waiting outside when the school day concludes."

Adam took a pause. "I would like you to give her another letter that I've recently drafted. Put the letter in a book and pass it to her that way. I'll be here tomorrow evening. The letter instructs her to respond to me. She is asked to put the answer to this correspondence and pass it back to you in the same book," he instructed.

"When Sister Catherine caught me passing the other letter to her, I was punished for a week, and I had to stay after school and write a composition on why one shouldn't pass notes in class," she said.

"I don't want you to get into any trouble, but it's very important that Geruese gets this message." He took a long pause and reached out and took her hand. "I want you to know that I'm depending on you."

He reached in this coat and took out the letter. Marguerite took the letter and slipped into one of the books that she had been carrying. "I'll see you tomorrow, that is, if I don't get caught by Sister Catherine," she said with a smile. She got up from the table and walked over and sat down with her friends.

Adam ordered a bottle of wine and watched the comings and goings of the patrons. Somehow he knew that having a life with Geruese could be fraught with a multitude of problems, but he believed that she was worth every difficulty that he might encounter in the foreseeable future.

About the same time as the day before, Adam entered the coffee shop in anticipation of meeting up with Marguerite. At almost the exact same time as the day before, she entered the coffee shop with her friends from school. When her eyes grew accustomed to the dim light, she spotted Adam and walked directly to his table. She sat at the same chair that she had occupied the day before.

She looked deep into Adam's eyes. "I wish I had a handsome officer that would be in love with me as you are with Geruese."

Ignoring that school girl comment, he said, "Well, did you deliver the letter?"

"Yes," she said.

"Did she write an answer to me?"

Marguerite opened her book and presented a sealed letter. Adam took the letter and studied the writing on the front of the envelope. He just sat there staring at the envelope.

Finally, Marguerite said, "Well, aren't you going to open it?"

"I want to, but I'm afraid of what message it might contain," he said as he took another drink of his wine. He tore open the envelope and attempted to read it in the dim light. There was a certain amount of ambient light coming through the door, so he turned the letter toward that light to enable him to read its contents. After several seconds, he dropped the letter on the table. Marguerite picked up the letter and gave it a fast glance. Adam snatched it away from her.

"I hope the two of you know what you're doing. Geruese is still a ward of her father, and if she does what she says she is willing to do, you may be arrested."

"I'm willing to take that chance. When you see her at school tomorrow, tell her that I will be waiting in a carriage a half block down from her house tomorrow evening at midnight. Tell her to pack a small suitcase and be ready to travel."

Facetiously, she said, "If for some reason Geruese doesn't arrive at the prescribed time, I would be willing to take her place. My father would be glad to get rid of me."

Smiling at her jest, he said, "I'll keep that in mind."

Adam leaned into her and kissed her cheek. "Thank you for delivering the letter and coming here this evening with the reply. You're a good friend," he said as he stood to signal her to leave so he could be alone. Marguerite left the table and walked over to her friends and sat down.

Adam began to make plans for the next day. There was going to be a lot to do and he wouldn't overlook any of the details.

The first item he had to deal with was to get an extended leave from his military duties. If he just left without filing the proper paper work, that would be desertion and would result in a jail sentence. Adam decided that he would inform his commanding officer that due to family problems, he would need an extended leave of absence.

He suddenly remembered his cousin, Emilie Tautou. She was living in Northern Spain and had dropped out of society five years ago to become an artist. Two years ago, right after he graduated from the military academy, he had spent two weeks with Cousin Emilie. She had two small houses on the property where she lived, one of which she didn't use. He was confident that she would allow him to live there for a period of time. Emilie led a Bohemian life style, and Adam was sure that she would not be adverse to a man and woman living together out of wedlock.

Adam would have to make a reservation with a carriage service to take them to Oviedo, the capital of the Asturias Province. *Once we meet at midnight, the carriage can take us there in a day's travel,* he thought.

Early the next morning, Adam met with his commanding officer. Against his better judgment, he told an untruth by requesting an indefinite leave from duty due to a family emergency. He outlined the fact that his father has passed away and his brother, who was running the estate, needed his help dealing with the multitude of operations. The commanding officer was sympathetic to his request and granted him the leave of absence. Once he left the military base, he went in search of a company that leased carriages. As he was speaking with the carriage company owner, he noticed a carriage for sale. He inquired about the price of the carriage, and after some negotiations and the cost of a horse, they agreed upon a price. Adam now had a mode of transportation.

Adam still had nine thousands livres that his brother had given him as his inheritance. He calculated that it was enough money to support Geruese and himself until she reached the age of majority. At that point he reasoned they could marry, return to Paris, and he could resume his military career.

Several minutes before midnight, Adam moved his carriage down the street from where Geruese lived with her father. As he passed the house, he took note that the house was in complete darkness. He continued down the street for several yards and brought the carriage to a stop. There was a full moon that night, and the top of his carriage was in the down position allowing the moon light to flood its interior. He looked at his pocket watch; it was one minute after midnight. He heard someone walking on the sidewalk and heading in his direction. When he turned, he was relieved to see Geruese a few feet from the carriage carrying a small bag.

Adam climbed out of the carriage and took her into his arms. They kissed; he relieved her of the bag that she was carrying and put it in the back of the carriage. He helped her onto the carriage seat, and then he moved around the other side and boarded. Adam had planned the route out of Paris. He began to drive the carriage with a sense of urgency. It was imperative that they be out of Paris before dawn when Geruese's father discovered her absence.

It was midmorning before Adam believed it was safe to stop. He located an inn to get something to eat. They only stayed at the inn long enough to have some breakfast and purchase food for the rest of the trip to Oviedo.

It was getting dark as they drove down the country road that led to Emilie's houses. In the main house a light could be seen through a window illuminating it's interior. Adam pulled up alongside the main door and brought the carriage to a complete stop. He got out of the carriage and walked around to the other side and helped Geruese down. He knocked on the door. Several seconds passed before Emilie stood before them.

"Adam, what are you doing here?" Emilie inquired.

"Let us in and I'll explain," he answered.

Emilie opened the door wide to allow them entrance. She directed them to a table and had them sit down. She placed some bread, cheese, and a bottle of wine before them. As they sat and ate, Adam explained that Geruese and he intended to be married. He said as soon as she reached the age of majority, they would move ahead with the marriage. In the meantime, they needed a place to hide from her father who was against their entering into the union of holy matrimony.

Emilie sat and listened to Adam explain his position. After she asked several questions about their future plans, she agreed to help them. They were welcome to live in the other house on the property until Geruese became legally out of her father's reach.

They were both exhausted from their trip from Paris; so, Adam requested that they be excused to retire for the night. Emilie took a lighted lantern and led Adam and Geruese to a small house several yards from the main. She opened the door and entered while Adam and Geruese waited for her to light some candles. Once an area was illuminated, Adam and Geruese, hand in hand, stepped inside.

The little house was small, but efficient. There were three rooms, the main room which was the largest, a kitchen area and bedroom with two small beds. "I don't have this house stocked with food, but I would like you to come over tomorrow morning for breakfast. I would also like you to dine with me until we can get you some supplies from the town," she said.

Adam said, "We don't want to be any trouble, Emilie, and I appreciate everything you're offering. I will go to town first thing tomorrow and get what we need for sustenance." He embraced Emilie.

"I'm going to leave now to allow the two of you to get some rest. I know that you must be exhausted from your trip. I'll see you in the morning." Emilie crossed to the door and let herself out.

Adam and Geruese stood alone in the middle of the room. Adam crosses to her and they embraced. After several seconds, as he crossed to the table and picked up a lighted candle, he said, "Take this and go into the bedroom and change into your night clothes. I'll wait here until you are presentable."

She took the candle, picked up her small bag and went into the bedroom. Adam wandered around the room and then he inspected the kitchen area. After a few minutes, Geruese opened the bedroom door and said, "I've changed." She moved back into the bedroom. Adam crossed to the bedroom and entered.

After a moment, observing her in her night clothes, "I think we have to talk," he said as he began to remove his clothes. "I've been giving this a lot of thought, and I want you to understand that I love you very much. I can't tell you how much I want to make love to you, but we have to practice self-control. We

12

are both Catholics, and we know it's a sin if we have a physical relationship out of wedlock. As long as we are together is enough for me at this time. As soon as you turn eighteen, we'll go into town and make arrangements at the church to be married."

Geruese stood frozen in the middle of the room and digested what Adam had just stated to her. After a long moment, she moved to one of the small beds, pulled back the blankets, and slid underneath.

Adam removed a nightgown from his bag and put it on. He then crossed to the small bed where Geruese was supine and sat on its side. He leaned in and kissed her. "Good night, my love, and get a good night's sleep. I'll see you first thing in the morning." After he kissed her, he then crossed back to the other small bed, climbed in and within minutes they were both asleep.

Back in Paris, when Geruese's father learned that his daughter had eloped with Adam he was furious. He contacted the Lieutenant General de Gendarme, who happened to be his friend since they were students at the prestigious Paris Academy. He gave Lieutenant General Berleand a list of names of young women that Geruese was friends with at school.

That very day, Berleand went to the school and interviewed the Mother Superior who informed him about Sister Catherine intercepting a letter being passed to Geruese from Marguerite. Geruese's father was familiar with the letter since it had been sent to his house by the school officials. Marguerite was the first name on Berleand's list to interview.

Berleand had Marguerite taken from class and escorted to a small room adjacent to the Mother Superior's office. Sitting at a table, when Marguerite entered the room, was a very stern Berleand, Mother Superior, and Geruese's father. They had her sit down facing these three intimidating individuals.

Berleand began the interview, "Is your name Marguerite Guilliot?"

"Yes Monsieur, that is correct."

Berleand continued, "Are you aware, Mademoiselle Guilliot, that it's a crime, punishable by imprisonment for assisting someone committing a crime?"

Marguerite took an awkward pause and then she said, "I haven't assisted anyone with committing a crime, Monsieur."

"Did you or did you not carry and pass notes from Monsieur Daulac to Mademoiselle Jovet on several occasions?"

"Yes Monsieur, but I wasn't made aware of the contents of those letters."

Berleand pressed her further, "Did you know that Mademoiselle Jovet was planning to elope with Monsieur Daulac? Remember, Mademoiselle, if you don't tell me everything that you know, you will become an accomplice and can go to jail."

Marguerite looked across the table at these three threatening individuals and was aware that if she didn't tell everything she knew about this situation, her life could be ruined. After a moment of silence, she said, "Geruese told me, the day before she left, that Adam was going to meet her at midnight and they were going to elope. She said that he would be waiting outside her house around midnight in a carriage."

Berleand continued, "And where were they intending to run off to?"

Marguerite looked down at the table knowing that she was betraying Geruese confidence. "Monsieur, if I tell you where they were planning to go Geruese will never speak to me again."

"If you don't tell me and you go to jail, she'll never speak to you again either," he said with a stern pitch to his voice. "I'm not going to ask you again, but think carefully about what you are about to say."

Marguerite began to sob. She knew that if she told him Geruese would never forgive her. On the other hand, she didn't want to go to jail for keeping silent. She justified that she hadn't promised Geruese that she wouldn't reveal her whereabouts. She had to tell him. "Geruese told me that Adam had a cousin in Oviedo, Spain, who had two houses on her property, and they were going to stay in one of them until she became eighteen years old, and then they were going to a church in Oviedo and getting married."

"And what was this cousin's name?" he asked

"I just remember the last name. It was Tautou, I believe."

Berleand looked at the Mother Superior and Geruese's father and then he smiled. And then he looked back at Marguerite and said, "Thank you, Mademoiselle; you've been extremely helpful and cooperative. You may leave."

Marguerite stood and asked the Mother Superior, "May I go back to class now, Sister?"

"Go, my child," she directed.

Marguerite slowly walked the length of the room and left.

After Marguerite closed the door, Berleand said to Geruese's father, "I will send two of my men to Oviedo today. They will have orders to request the cooperation of the Oviedo gendarmes and explain to them that this man, Adam Daulac, enticed this underage girl to come to Spain with him for immoral purposes. I will provide my men with extradition papers to be given to the Spanish authorities. I will also contact Lieutenant Daulac's Commander and inform him of the action we will be taking against one of his officers."

After Adam and Geruese had breakfast with Emilie, they took their carriage and drove into town to purchase food and other essentials. When they arrived in the city, the first building they noticed was the Oviedo Cathedral. They parked the carriage and entered the Cathedral to observe the beautiful decorations of its interior. It was noted that the walls were lined with gold that had been sent to Spain by the Conquistadores.

As they sat silently in a pew admiring the beauty of the Cathedral's interior, a "Pere" came out of the Sacristy. He observed the couple sitting in the pew in the back of the Cathedral and walk toward them. "I am Pere Bastien. May I be of some assistance to you?"

Adam said, "We were just sitting here, Padre, enjoying the beauty of this wonderful Cathedral."

"Are the two of you residents of this city or are you just visiting?" he inquired.

"We are just visiting, Padre. We would like to get married in Oviedo in a few months before returning to Paris. I am a Lieutenant in the Army and must eventually return to my military duties."

"When you decide to take the vows of the sacrament of matrimony come and see me. I would be happy to perform the ceremony," Pere Bastien said.

"Thank you, Padre, we will seriously consider your offer," Adam countered.

Pere Bastien turned walked back toward the Sacristy and disappeared from sight. Adam and Geruese left the Cathedral, and then drove their carriage to the market in the center of the city.

When they arrived back at their house at Emilie's little compound, they prepared lunch from the food they had purchased. The rest of the afternoon was spent exploring the area. There was a long road that led to a large hill that overlooked the city. They climbed the hill and sat transcending with the nature that surrounded them. They spoke of their plans for the future and Adam was anxious to show Geruese his little house on the Left Bank. Geruese was five months before she became the age of majority and it was imperative they wait before they married, otherwise, her father could declare the union null and void.

That evening when they returned to their little house, Emilie had left a note attached to their door inviting them to her house for dinner at seven that evening. They hurriedly changed their clothes and walked the short distance to Emilie's house.

Emilie greeted them with an open bottle of wine. She poured three glasses and had them sit at the table where the meal was going to be served in a few minutes. Adam told Emilie that they had explored the area and was very impressed with the surroundings.

Emilie served baked duck and variety of vegetables. After dinner they sat and talked until nearly midnight as they drank three bottles of wine. Eventually, Adam and Geruese excused themselves and returned to their little house. They were both exhausted from the day's activities and went right to bed. Within minutes they were asleep.

Back in Paris, Berleand had assigned three of his gendarme officers to go to Oviedo and carry the extradition notice for Adam and Geruese to the Oviedo officials. These men arrived in the early hours of the morning and went directly to the Cities Public Facility. With the information that Marguerite had provided them, they knew the name of Adam cousin. When they gave the name, "Tautou," to the Oviedo officials, they were aware of where she lived.

The Oviedo police and the Paris gendarmes drove immediately in three carriages to Emilie's compound. When they arrived at the little house Adam and Geruese were having breakfast. Emilie was sitting by the window when she heard the carriages. She looked out and saw the procession of carriages approaching. Before she could reach the house where Adam and Geruese were lodging, the men in the carriages were out and had surrounded the house. One of the men intercepted Emilie and escorted her back to her house.

The men were pounding on the door of the small house. Adam answered the door and was immediately taken into custody. They cuffed his hands and placed him into one of the carriages. Another man took Geruese by the arm and placed her into another. One of the Oviedo policia sternly told Emilie that she could be prosecuted for harboring fugitives. He told her a decision would be made by the Oviedo officials if charges were going to be brought. She was warned not to leave the area.

The Paris gendarmes thanked the Oviedo policia for their cooperation and their two carriages began their trek back to Paris. Adam and Geruese were now going to have to face the consequences for their actions.

Two

*W*hen they arrived in Paris, it was early morning. They were taken directly to the gendarme headquarters. Adam was placed in a cell and Geruese was escorted into a private room to await her father.

After a short period of time, Berleand came to the cell where Adam was being held. After a moment of looking at him through the bars he said, "You know young man that you are in a lot of trouble. I have sent a messenger to your commanding officer and asked him to come here immediately. I am going to turn you over to the military and let them deal with you."

Two hours passed before one of the guards brought Adam something to eat. He was starving since he hadn't eaten anything substantial since breakfast the morning before. He wondered if Geruese was still in the headquarters, or if her father had whisked her away.

After he finished his breakfast, and as he was drinking a cup of coffee, he looked up and saw Captain Roussel staring at him through the bars. Captain Damien Roussel had been in the army for about ten years and was Adam's commanding officer. Adam put down the coffee cup and walked to the bars opposite Damien.

"Adam, what on earth did you do? I've been told that you kidnapped a seventeen-year-old girl and took her out of the country for immoral purposes."

"Sir, that isn't exactly the truth. Yes, I took a seventeen-year-old girl to Spain, but she went freely with me. We're in love and want to be together. In five months, she will reach an age of majority and we intend to be married."

"Why didn't you just wait those five months instead of doing what you so foolishly did?"

"Her father was intent on not allowing her to see me. He had intercepted a letter that I wrote requesting her to meet me at a coffee house. From that time on, I was not allowed to come to her house and court her. We both had a desperate need to be together, so I made arrangements to take her to Spain where my cousin lives. Although we were together the entire time, I respected her purity and nothing sexual transpired."

"Of course, there's the fact that you told me an untruth to get time away from your military duties. How could I ever trust anything you say in the future?" He took a slight pause and then he said, "I am going to recommend you for a court martial to the Colonel. I must tell you, I am very disappointed in your conduct. I have brought three soldiers with me to escort you back to the base. The gendarme will turn you over to us in a few minutes." He turned, walked away and out the door at the end of the hallway.

Adam was taken to the Military Base ten miles north of Paris and confined to a barrack. He was to stay there until a court martial was convened. For the next two weeks, he only saw the guards who brought him food twice a day. At the end of the second week, his brother Hamnet came to see him.

Adam was taken to a small room with a table and two chairs facing one another. As he entered the room his brother was already seated at the table. Adam sat down opposite his brother and neither one said anything for several seconds. Finally, Hamnet broke the silence. "What in the name of God were you thinking to take an underage girl out of the country without the permission of her father?"

"I know what it looks like, but she went willingly with me. We're in love and intend to get married in the very near future," Adam countered.

"I spoke with her father. Although he is very upset with both of you, he only wants you out of his daughter's life. He's aware that you don't have an inheritance, and he is convinced that you could never support his daughter in the manner she is accustomed. For the time being, she is no longer in the city and has been sent to a Convent in Normandy to continue her education. She will remain there until she reaches the age of twenty-one."

"Her father doesn't have the right to keep her confined after she passes the age of eighteen," he reminded Hamnet.

After a few seconds, Hamnet said, "He may keep her locked away indefinitely if she is considered mentally deficient. Her father had a doctor friend sign the necessary papers. She will not be released from the Convent until that same doctor signs a release. My advice to you, my brother, is to forget this young lady and pray the military will be lenient with you for your poor behavior."

Adam was stunned. He put his hands to his face and put his head down on the table.

Hamnet told him that he had spoken with the colonel who would be conducting his hearing. "I assured the colonel I would put in a good word with the King if he were to treat you leniently."

Adam raised his head and looked directly at Hamnet. "I don't want to stay in the army any longer. If I'm released, I will resign my commission and leave Paris."

"Don't do anything rash. It may take some time, but you can still have a rewarding career if you admit at your hearing that what you did was a lack of good judgment and it will never happen again."

Hamnet stood and extended his hand. "Take care, my brother, and I'll be praying for you."

Adam took his hand and they shook. Adam turned and returned to his barrack.

Another three weeks passed. Adam was finally notified that his hearing was set for the next day.

That afternoon a guard informed him that he had a visitor. He took him to the same room where he had previously met his brother. When he opened the door, he saw Marguerite seated at the table.

For a moment, he was completely surprised to see her sitting in front of him. He sat down. Several moments passed in silence. "What are you doing here?" he inquired.

"I think about you often. I had to be careful coming here though. I wouldn't want my parents to know that I had visited you. All the parents at the school believe that you are a child molester. But I know different. I know that Geruese and you are in love, but no one else sees it that way. As far as they are concerned, you are a grown man who influenced a child to go to another country for immoral purposes."

"You know that isn't true. You were good friends with Geruese, and you had conversations with me on numerous occasions. I'm sorry that she is only seventeen, and I would give anything if she were just a little older. I want you to know that while we were away in Spain nothing happened between the two of us. All we did the whole time was talk and spend time together. And now, I've learned that she has been committed for mental treatment and it's entirely my fault. I should have waited those five short months before we made a move to elope."

She reached her hand across the table as Adam took hers in his grip, and they sat for a long time looking into one another's eyes. "I intend to go and see her in a day or two. Is there anything you would like me to say to her?" she asked.

"Yes, tell her that I love her, and I will always love her no matter where the two of us eventually wind up. When they release me, eventually, I intend to leave Paris and France. I don't know where I'm going at this moment, but it will be far away. Tell her that we must try to forget one other. As long as she insists on being with me, they will never release her from that institution. Promise me you'll tell her that."

"I promise," Marguerite said.

"Thank you for coming here today, you have been a good friend," he said as he stood and left the room.

Back in his barrack, Adam spent the rest of the evening preparing for his hearing scheduled for the next day. After several hours of attempting to put together a defense, structuring one that was logical became impossible. He decided to throw himself on the mercy of the tribunal. The truth was simple: he had allowed his love and emotions to dictate a careless behavior. He would assure them that he would never allow his emotions to rule his common sense in the future. Furthermore, he was sorry for misrepresenting his reason for getting additional leave from his military duties.

At nine o'clock the next morning, Adam was led across the yard to the administration building. He was taken into a large room and sat in a chair facing a long table. A few minutes later, three uniformed officers entered the room and stood at the table. Adam stood at attention when the men appeared. There was a colonel and two captains. Everyone was asked to be seated except Adam. Adam was required to stand and face the officers while the charges were read.

The colonel began the procedure by reading the charges that Adam was being accused.

"Lieutenant Adam Daulac, charge one: you are being accused of lying to your commanding officer for the purpose of being excused from your military duties. Charge two: you are accused of taking an underage female across the border of another country for immoral purposes. How do you plead?" the colonel asked.

After a moment of digesting the charges Adam responded, "Sir, I am guilty of the first charge. I did in fact tell an untruth to my commanding officer. I needed more time to put into effect a plan to be with my beloved. As to the second charge, that is absolutely false. Geruese and I are in love and we wanted to be together. But Sirs, I honored her purity the entire time. The plan was to wait until she became the age of majority and marry. If she is questioned, she will tell you I conducted myself as a gentleman and officer the entire time we were together in Spain."

The colonel looked first to his right and then to his left. "Gentlemen," he said, "let us retire to the next room and decide this case." They all stood and went into an adjacent room.

Adam was returned to his cell to await their decision. He concluded it shouldn't take long. It was late afternoon before he was called back to the hearing room. Adam stood in front of his chair as the three officers took their places behind the large table. The officers sat down and Adam was requested to remain standing. The colonel had a document in front of him that he referred to as he spoke. "Lieutenant Adam Daulac, you have been charged with two counts. First, that you lied to a commanding officer to relieve you from your military duties. The second offense states that you took an underage female out of France for immoral purposes. We had the opportunity of interviewing Mademoiselle Geruese Jovet at the Convent where she is incarcerated. She swore to us that the entire time the two of you were together that no sexual activity occurred. Therefore, the charge that you took this young woman out of France for immoral purposes is dismissed. However, on the first charge that you lied to a commanding officer to be relieved of your military duties has proved to be true as admitted by your testimony. You are hereby found guilty of an action unbecoming an officer in the French army. Sentencing will be forthcoming tomorrow morning at nine o'clock. This tribunal is concluded." The officers stood and left the room.

Adam spent the rest of the day and evening wondering what sentence would be passed down. The most important part of this unfortunate situation was the fact that he was cleared of the immoral accusation. The worst thing he was guilty of was the fact that he fell in love with a young woman who had not reached the age of majority. No matter what happened, he would always love her even though they would never be together.

The next morning, Adam was escorted to the hearing room for sentencing. When the door opened only the colonel took his place at the table. The two captains who had previously assisted him were absent. Adam stood before the colonel to await his destiny.

Once again the colonel referred to the document he was holding in front of him. "Lieutenant Adam Daulac, you have been found guilty of lying to a commanding officer for personal gain. Therefore, it is the decision of the tribunal that there is no place for an officer in the French army who will not tell the truth at all times. From this moment, you are relieved of your commission and dishonorably discharged from the army. I would recommend that you spend the rest of your life atoning for this reckless error, and to do something that will make amends for your crime. Find something to do with your life that will make your country proud of you in the end. You are hereby released from custody."

The colonel stood and left the room. Adam was escorted back to the barrack to retrieve the few personal things that he had stored there.

The military base was about two miles from his lodgings on the Left Bank. To make matters worse, it began to rain. *A perfect day to be dishonorably discharged from the army,* he thought.

After an hour and a half of walking in the rain, Adam finally arrived at his lodgings. As he approached his door, he noticed a note wedged between the door and the door frame. When he opened the note, it was from Marguerite and it was dated the day before. He wondered how she knew where he lived. In their several conversations, his domicile was never mentioned.

The note informed him that she would be at the coffee shop every day after school. She had been allowed to visit Geruese at the Convent and she had a message for him from her. Adam knew that if he was going to get this whole situation behind him, it was imperative that he begin immediately to put Geruese out of his mind. In the mental state that he was in, getting a message from Geruese through Marguerite would not be helpful.

Adam thought back about what the colonel said to him after he had passed his sentence. "Do something with your life to make amends and make your country proud of you in the end."

I must leave Paris, he thought.

He began to pack his bag with only his civilian clothing. The uniforms would be left behind. There was a company that booked public transportation to various cities nearby. The family home was located in Chantilly about thirty miles from Paris. He continued to pack his suitcase. *I should talk this situation over with Hamnet and see what he advises me to do with the rest of my life,* he thought.

He left the lodgings and walked the twelve blocks to the area where the carriages were for hire. As luck would have it, there were three other people looking for a ride to Chantilly as well. The carriage could accommodate four, so the carriage driver couldn't have been happier to have a full load.

The road to Chantilly was nothing more than two tracks dug out of the mud and dirt. To say the ride was bumpy would be an understatement. His companions on the trip were an elderly couple enroute to take care of their sick son and a young woman about his age who had been recently widowed. She had lost her husband to smallpox, which was raging throughout the City of Paris at the time.

The journey to Chantilly took three and a half hours. When they arrived, he hired another carriage to take him to his old homestead. As the carriage rode slowly down the road that led to the family estate, he saw his sister sitting on the porch of the house where he had spent his youth. When she saw the carriage approaching, she ran into the house to summon Hamnet. The front door opened and both of them came out onto the porch to see who was about to visit.

When Adam stepped out of the carriage, Pauline was excited to see him. On the other hand, Hamnet looked somewhat surprised. Pauline ran down the steps and into his arms.

"I'm so glad to see you," she whispered in his ear as she hugged him tight.

"I see you must have won your appeal with the military tribunal," Hamnet said.

"Not exactly, but we can discuss that a little latter." He moved Pauline back to kiss her on the cheek. With his arm around her waist, they walked up the steps past Hamnet and into the house. Hamnet followed behind them.

Hamnet said, "Please sit down, you must be very tired. Would you like something to drink?"

Pauline sat across from Adam as Hamnet opened a bottle of wine that was displayed on a table in the dining room. He poured a glass for each of them and returned to the living room. They sat in silence for a short period of time sipping their wine.

Adam broke the silence. "I have been dishonorably discharged from the army. The charge of taking a young woman who hasn't reached the age of majority for immoral purposes out of the country was dismissed. But I was found guilty of being dishonest in applying for leave from my military duties. I know what I did was wrong and I deserve the sentence that's been imposed on me."

Hamnet took another sip of his wine and then he said, "So, what are you going to do now? Being in the army was something that you always aspired."

Adam looked over at Pauline who was quietly sobbing. Turning toward Hamnet he said, "I was hoping that you could give me council. I'm lost without my military career."

Hamnet took a long pause and then he said, "Do you remember Acelet Desmarais?"

"Yes, of course. He taught for a short time at the primary school where I attended," he said.

"He was here about a month ago on his way to Paris. He had just returned from New France on a missionary assignment. Acelet was ordained a Jesuit priest some time ago and spent a year at a Huron mission in Northern New France. According to Acelet,

New France is wide open for someone like you to begin a new life and take advantage of your military experience and talents. I think that you should consider going there for a time; if that experience doesn't offer you opportunities, take a ship back to France."

Adam thought about what he had said. "Will you make arrangements for a letter of introduction from the King?"

"Yes, but it will necessary for you to change your name. The King will not, I'm sure, give a letter of introduction to someone who was dishonorably discharged from the army."

Hamnet thought for several seconds before he said, "Change your name to 'Adam Dollard.' I'll draft a résumé for Monsieur Dollard using your educational background and say that you were not accepted into the army due to your strong religious beliefs, and had for a time considered becoming a priest. With your academic background, studying at the prestigious French Military Academy at Coetquidan and having trained in military science, your presence would be an asset to the colony of New France." Hamnet turned to Adam and said, "From this day forward your sur name will no longer be Daulac, but Dollard."

Hamnet took a slight pause and then he asked, "Is that acceptable to you?"

"When I go to New France, I will do everything within my power to make my family and country proud of me," Adam said as he held out his glass for a refill of the wine.

Over the next few months, Adam continued living at the country estate while Hamnet prepared all the necessary paperwork to be submitted to the King for an introduction to the Governor of New France, Jean de Lauson.

After the paperwork had been completed, it was submitted to the King. A few months later, a courier arrived with an envelope displaying the royal seal and addressed to Monsieur Dollard. It was an introduction of Adam Dollard to the Governor of New France from Louis XIV, King of France.

Within the past few weeks, Hamnet had been expecting this letter of introduction any day, so he began to check with the port of Calais to see which ships was anticipating sailing to New France. Several Jesuits from the monastery a few miles away were going to be sending a few missionaries there. They had booked passage on a ship named Grand Anglais that was scheduled to sail in the spring. She was in dry dock having repairs, but it was expected that by the end of April the ship would be launched and ready to sail. It was now the end of March and the Jesuits were packed and ready to make the trip to Calais.

Dollard packed a small bag and made arrangements to leave with the Jesuits. The carriage arrived with the three Jesuits aboard. They were Pere's Claude Lalemant, Jean de Brebeuf, and Jacques Bruyas. They were a quiet a diverse group overall. Pere Brebeuf was the most friendly and questioned Adam at length as to why he was traveling to New France. "Are you interested in fur trapping, sir?" he inquired.

Adam told him that he knew nothing about trapping furs.

"So if you're not interested in fur trapping, why would a man like yourself, twenty-two years old and educated, be interested with settling in New France?" he questioned.

The questioning along these lines continued for several minutes until Adam had had enough. He said, "If you must know, Padre, my main reason for traveling to New France is to take an Iroquois bride and convert to their heathen ways."

The two Jesuits who had been witness to this interrogation finally dissolved into uncontrollable laughter.

Pere Brebeuf didn't ask any more questions for the rest of the trip. There was an hour stopover in Attas to water the horses and give the passengers a respite. The three Jesuits and Dollard went to an Inn that served lunch. The Jesuits and Adam each had a glass of wine with the soup that was served. Dollard questioned the Jesuit Lalemant about his plans once he arrived in New France.

"There is a Huron Mission in the north of New France, St. Ignace, several hundred miles from the city of Quebec. I've been told by missionaries who have previously been to New France, that we can make arrangements with either fur traders or Algonquian natives to take us there up the St. Lawrence River, and then from there to the Ottawa River," he said as the other two Jesuits nodded their heads in agreement.

The coach driver came into the Inn and summoned them to depart. They had another four-hour trip ahead before reaching their destination.

Adam was extremely tired. He hadn't been sleeping well at night anticipating his journey to New France, and what he was going to do once he arrived. He dozed off once the carriage got underway.

As they approached the city limits of Calais, one of the Jesuits nudged him out of his slumber. "We are almost at our destination," the Jesuit said.

Adam opened his eyes as they were passing through the small seaport town. The carriage driver was instructed to take them directly to the docked ship, the Grand Anglais. The waterfront was illuminated with lamps hanging on poles several yards apart. There were several large ships docked against the half-mile-long pier. The carriage driver drove slowly down the pier reading the names of the various ships. Finally, he stopped the carriage and announced that they had reached their destination. The three Jesuits and Adam stepped out of the carriage and walked around to the back. There they released the straps that were holding the luggage in place. Once they identified their suitcase, they walked up the gangplank in single file. Adam was the last one to board the ship.

The captain of the Grand Anglais, Matthieu Severin, greeted them as they stepped onto the deck. He directed his first mate to show the passengers to their respective quarters. The group of four was going to be divided in pairs. Adam was going to share a room with the Jesuit Lalemant. The Jesuits Brebeuf and Bruyas had been to New France once before and lived among the Huron's. This was going to be a first visit to New France for Adam and Lalemant and they were anxious at the possibilities.

When the Jesuits and Adam reach New France, Bruyas would be remaining at Quebec administering the sacraments and teaching at a school for novitiate nuns. Lalemant was to travel up the St. Lawrence with Brebeuf and report to the Huron missions to relieve the two Jesuits who had been there for three years. Adam was to serve at the will of the governor of Quebec, Jean de Lauson.

The Grand Anglais remained in port until the morning of the fourth day. Four nuns boarded the ship for the trip to New France and supplies were loaded for the three thousand-mile journey. On the fifth day with the afternoon tide, the lines attached to the Grand Anglais were released and she slipped out into the harbor with her topsails raised. Slowly, she navigated toward the mouth of the harbor and into the Atlantic.

On the first evening, the Jesuits and Dollard dined in with Captain Severin. The four nun passengers were not allowed to socialize with the men. The captain had them served dinner in their quarters.

After a few days, the nuns were allowed out of their quarters and stood for a period of time at the ship's rail to get some fresh air. Adam noticed two young nuns getting their daily dose of exercise. He hadn't spoken to a woman other than his sister, Pauline, since he had left the military compound. Adam had a need to hear a female voice. "Good morning, Soeurs," he said.

The nun closest to him shyly said, "Good morning, sir."

"Are you ladies excited about going to New France?" he inquired

"We are apprehensive, sir. We have heard good things and bad things as well. But we are on this earth to serve God. If our Order believes that we will do the most good in New France, then we accept that assignment with all the energy we have to accomplish our mission, and to save the souls of the savages," she announced with a determination in her young voice.

A silence fell over their conversation. Adam didn't have anything else to say. He had never conversed with a nun on an equal plane before. The nuns he had in primary school were teachers and not conversationalists.

The trip to New France for the most part was uneventful, except for the hurricane-type storm the Grand Anglais encountered halfway across the Atlantic. The nuns, like most of the passengers aboard, were all sick below deck. Being on deck during one of these storms could be lethal.

Two days later, the sun came out and seas calmed. When Adam came up on deck to get some much needed air, he observed the three nuns down on their knees thanking God for saving them from the raging seas.

A week later the captain informed everyone that they were entering the Gulf of St. Lawrence. He pointed out the whales breaking the waves as they sailed by. Captain Severin said it was the whales and fishing that brought the first Europeans to this body of water. Several hours later, the Grand Anglais sailed by the islands of St. Pierre and Miquelon, and eventually, they passed the largest island in the Gulf of St. Lawrence, Anticoati.

Once past that large island, the ship entered the mouth of the St. Lawrence River that Jacques Cartier sailed up over a hundred years before. The river began to narrow and there were many small islands to navigate around as they sailed the one hundred and thirty-five miles to their destination, Quebec.

All of the passengers were on deck for the last leg of this exciting trip. The nuns began to pray thanking god for delivering them safely to this foreign, undeveloped land. As they sailed along there were signs of land being cleared for farming. Periodically, a Frenchman felling a tree would stop from his work and wave at the passing ship.

It took two full days to navigate up this river, but on the morning of the third day, the Grand Anglais sailed around a large island (Ile d'Orleans) and into the St. Lawrence basin where it widened in front of Quebec City and its massive rock. The ship dropped its anchor about twenty-five yards off the shoreline. The cannons atop of the rock were fired to announce the arrival of a new ship in their harbor. Leading up to the upper city was a steep winding road. Many colonists, including the governor, several Jesuits, and nuns, had come down to the shoreline to welcome the passengers from France.

The captain of the Grand Anglais, as soon as the ship was securely anchored, ordered a barca (small boat) lowered for the three nuns, Jesuits, Adam, and two sailors to row them to the shore and the awaiting crowd. The Governor, Jean de Lauson, was the first to greet and welcome them to New France. Introductions were made all around and the small group made their way up the steep road to the upper city. Led by the governor, they made their way to his residence where they were treated to a late breakfast.

Everyone was seated around a large rectangular table. They were served eggs and pancakes with hot coffee and tea. Each of the nuns and Jesuits outlined to the governor the instructions they had been given by the heads of their respective Orders. Two of the nuns were to remain at Quebec City and work in their hospital as well as teach in the Catholic school once it was constructed. The young nun, whom Adam had spoken to at the ship's railing, was to travel to Trois Rivieres and assist in their hospital. Pere Bruyas was to assist the single Jesuit at the Catholic Church saying mass, visiting the sick and dying and converting the savages. Pere's Lalemant and Brebeuf were going to relieve the Jesuits currently administering the mission of St. Ignace among the Huron's in the upper north of New France.

After some extensive conversation as to their respective duties with their new assignments, the attention turned toward Adam Dollard. He had in his packet the letter of introduction to be presented to the governor. He took the letter from his packet and handed it to the governor. The governor took note of the royal seal and deferred reading it until he had a private audience with Adam.

The governor spent about an hour explaining to this group the mission of New France in great detail. When it was all broken down, there were three important missions for this new colony.

"First, it is the fur trade. Secondly, it is the conversion of the savages; and, thirdly, and most important, the exploration of the continent to search for a passage to the Orient," he said.

Eventually, the nuns excused themselves, and the governor had one of his servants lead them to the Convent at the top of the hill. The Jesuits and Adam remained with the governor, answering his many questions on the state of affairs in France. After several bottles of wine, the Jesuits were escorted to the Rectory next to the church that was under construction. Dollard remained while the governor opened the letter he had previously been given from the King.

The governor read the letter very carefully, looked up and smiled at Dollard and said, "Young man, the King has instructed me to use your military talents that will best serve New France."

He took a moment and then he said, "I have just the assignment for you. There is a small settlement, Ville-Marie, which is about one hundred and eighty miles up the St. Lawrence River from Quebec. There are less than three hundred French, Indian allies, one Jesuit, and four nuns that make up its population. The men and the Indians have a need to be trained in the art of war. They are under constant threat from the Iroquois. I would like you to go there and provide that training. From this moment on, you will hold the rank of Colonel in the army of New France."

Adam was surprised, and yet delighted, with this assignment. He was confident that the governor would eventually use his military experience, but he didn't think it would happen that soon.

"In two days, Soeur Marie, the youngest of the nuns who had just arrived, and two of the Jesuits will be traveling up the river as well. The nun will be going to Trois Rivieres where she will assist in a hospital. Pere's Lalemant and Brebeuf will travel with you to Ville-Marie. They will rest for a few days before they continue up to the Huron mission of St. Ignace. I will also send with you four Algonquian and four Huron to assist in guarding this human treasure." He took a moment for Adam to respond. "Do you have any questions?"

"No, your Excellency, I know exactly what you are requiring

of me, and I will fulfill my duties in a professional manner. Now, if you'll be so kind as to have one of your servants show me to my quarters, I would like to get some rest. I'm exhausted from the journey."

"Of course, I will have Pierre show you to your room."

The governor left the room, and moments later, Pierre arrived.

"Monsieur, if you'll follow me." Pierre led the way out of the room and up a stairway. They walked down the hall where there were half dozen doors on either side. Near the end of the hall the door on the right was slightly open. Pierre opened the door all the way and indicated to Adam that this was where he would be sleeping for the time being.

"Thank you, Pierre," Adam said.

"I'll be calling you for dinner in a few hours, sir."

Adam entered the room, placed his bag on the dresser, and collapsed on the bed. Adam dozed off. What seemed like a short time later, a knock was heard at the door? Adam dragged himself out of bed and opened the door.

"Sir, dinner will be served in a few minutes. You may want to freshen up before coming down," Pierre informed him.

"Thank you, Pierre, I'll be down in a few minutes," he replied. He closed the door and looked around the room. In the corner was a wash pan filled with water, a washcloth, and towel. He washed his face and hands, and from his bag he took a clean shirt and put it on.

When he believed he was presentable, he left the room, walked down the stairs and into the dining room. The table was set for six and he was the first one to arrive. Moments later, the governor, his aid Monsieur Le Maine, and the three Jesuits he had traveled with from France entered the room.

"Messieurs, please be seated," the governor commanded.

A waiter came into the room and filled each wine glass. After all the glasses were filled, the governor raised his glass and made a toast. "I toast that all of you arrived safely from France and we look forward to having you in our little colony. God save the King."

Everyone repeated, "God save the King."

Two waiters entered the room and began to serve the food. The meal consisted of roasted duck, fish, and variety of vegetables. There was some small talk during the dinner, but once it was completed, the governor began to give them a short history lesson.

"When the founder of New France, Samuel de Champlain, came here in the year 1604, he befriended the natives that were living on this very rock. Those natives were a group known as Algonquian. Among the original French colonists was a Jesuit by the name of La Roche. He had this unique ability to learn languages in a short time frame. Only days after they arrived, he had mastered all of the one hundred words in the Algonquian language and spoke it like a native. Monsieur Champlain had him question the Algonquians about the geography of the area. One of the missions of this settlement is to learn, if possible, a route through this land to the Orient. The Algonquians told Pere La Roche about these large bodies of water west and slightly south of their location. They told him that in the spring they were going on a war party against their mortal enemies, the Iroquois. So, on a sunny morning in May, Champlain and five of his heavily armed soldiers left Quebec with one hundred Algonquians to face and defeat this mysterious enemy. When they reached the Richelieu River, they paddled down for many miles until they reached a large lake. After two more days on the lake, they came to a rocky promontory where they made camp for night. In the morning, they carried their canoes and launched them into another lake. After paddling most of the day, they came upon a war party of Iroquois coming toward them from the opposite direction. The Algonquians had the French lay down in the canoes and out of sight of the Iroquois. After both sides exchanged many insults, each war party agreed to meet the next morning in battle along the shoreline. As the next day approached, Champlain had his men put on their light armor. They had at their side a sword and in their hand their harquebus. Each of the Frenchmen was in a separate canoe, and, as it grew light, they kept themselves hidden by covering themselves with an Indian robe. There were about two hundred Iroquois. Leading the Iroquois warriors was three of their chief's identified by their tall plumes. Some bore shields of wood and hide, and some were covered with a kind of armor made of tough twigs interlaced with a vegetable fiber. The Algonquians lined up facing the Iroquois, and then they called for Champlain and his men to come forward, which they did and faced the Iroquois warriors. When he saw them getting ready to shoot their arrows, Champlain and his men dropped their blankets, leveled their harquebus, which were loaded with four balls, and took straight aim at the three Iroquois chiefs and fired. They killed two and wounded one. The Iroquois were greatly astonished and frightened to see their men killed so quickly, in spite of their arrow-proof armor. Seeing their chief's dead, they abandoned the field and fled into the forest. The victory was complete. From that time until today, the Iroquois considers the French their mortal enemies," the governor concluded.

The governor took a slight pause before he said, "The purpose of that story is to give you all some background on how the war with the Iroquois began and continues to this day. That was more than fifty years ago."

There was a silence around the table and on several of their faces a look of concern.

"I would like to thank you for that detailed history lesson, Governor Lauson. It gives everyone at this table an insight as to why the Iroquois hate the French with such a vengeance. After all these years, hasn't anyone tried to parley with them?" Dollard inquired.

"There are five different tribes south of here and they stretch from east to west. The closest tribe to us is the Mohawks. We have negotiated peace with them in the past, but they are influenced by the other tribes and eventually broke that peace. They are also conducting a war of extermination on our allies, the Huron's. That conflict, I understand, has been going on for hundreds of years. We have sent our Jesuits among them to negotiate a peace and convert them to the true religion, but mostly, they wind up in their fires," the governor said.

The governor took a slight pause. "I just want you to know the danger you will experiencing tomorrow when you begin your journey up the St. Lawrence. The Iroquois have been camped around Quebec and have harassed us for years. They can come out of anywhere, so you must be on your constant guard."

The governor continued, "I would like to tell you a brief story about how Ville-Marie began, and its governor to this day oversees the little settlement. The little colony of about thirty hardy Frenchmen lead by a commandant, Maisonneuve, and assisted by two ladies, Madame de la Peltrie and Mademoiselle Mance. They arrived on an island in the St. Lawrence and they called it Ville-Marie. Immediately they fell to their work. Maisonneuve hewing down the first tree and labored with such goodwill, that their tents were soon enclosed with a strong palisade. A alter was constructed and covered by a provisional chapel, built in the Huron mode of bark. Soon afterward, their canvas habitations were supplanted by solid structures of wood, and the feeble germ of a city began to take root. The Iroquois had not discovered them yet, nor did they until they had ample time to fortify themselves. After attending mass on a Sunday, they would stroll at their leisure over the adjacent meadow and in the shade of the bordering forest where the grass was gay with wild flowers, and the branches fluttered with songs of the many strange birds. The day of the Assumption of the Virgin was celebrated with befitting solemnity. There was a mass in their bark chapel, then a Te Deum: public instruction of certain Algonquians who chanced to be at Ville-Marie. The first summer passed prosperously, but with the winter their faith was put to a rude test. In December, there was a rise in the St. Lawrence, threatening to sweep away in a night the results of all their labor. They fell into prayer. Maisonneuve planted a wooden cross in face of the advancing deluge, first making a vow that should the peril be averted, he, Maisonneuve, would bear another cross on his shoulders up the neighboring mountain and place it on the summit. The vow seemed in vain. The flood still rose, filled the fort ditch, swept the foot of the palisade, and threatened to sap the magazine; but here it stopped, and presently began to recede, till at length it had withdrawn within its lawful channel and Ville-Marie was safe. Now it remained to fulfill the promise from which such happy results had proceeded. Maisonneuve set his men at work to clear a path through the forest to the top of the mountain. A large cross was made and on the sixth of January, the Jesuit Du Petrie led the way with artisans, and soldiers, to the destined spot. When Maisonneuve finally arrived, he planted the huge cross at the summit of the mountain as he promised to do. Peace and harmony reigned within the little fort. At the end of

August, 1643, a vessel arrived at Ville-Marie carrying supplies and additional Frenchmen. Their vessel had passed safely and its arrival filled the colonists with joy. Shortly thereafter, a hospital was constructed and enclosed with a strong palisade, and, in time of danger, a part of the garrison was detailed to defend it. It was the hope of the French to form an agricultural settlement of Native Americans in the neighborhood of Ville-Marie, and they spared no exertion to this end, giving them tools, and aiding them in the fields. They might have succeeded, but for the Iroquois who eventually discovered them. Now the Iroquois hovered about them, harassed them with petty attacks, and again and again drove the Algonquians in terror from their camps. When ten Algonquians were chased by a party of them, they made haste for the friendly settlement as a safe asylum, Ville-Marie. The Iroquois reconnoitered the place and went back to their towns with the news."

The governor sighed and took a brief pause. And then he continued, "From that time forth the colonists have had no peace. There are no more excursions for fishing and hunting, no more Sunday strolls in the woods and meadows, and they are constantly on their guard. The men go armed to work and return at the sound of a bell, marching in a compact body, prepared for an attack. At Ville-Marie, it is usually dangerous to pass beyond the ditch of the fort or the palisades of the hospital. Sometimes a solitary warrior will lie hidden for days, without sleep and almost without food, behind a log in the forest, or in a dense thicket, watching like a lynx for some rash straggler. Sometimes parties of a hundred or more made ambuscades nearby, and send a few of their number to lure out the soldiers by a petty attack and a flight. This is what has been going on for the past fifteen years at Ville-Marie, and this is why, Monsieur Dollard, your services are direly needed."

The Governor had his servant break out three more bottles of wine and served it to his guests. Everyone at the table was now well aware of what they were confronted, and the dangers that existed in this wilderness that was called New France. Everyone, including the Jesuits, had several more glasses of wine before they retired for the night.

Three

The morning after arriving in Quebec, the French group including the two Jesuits and the nun, Soeur Adelaise, arrived at the governor's palace. There they met with Dollard and were escorted into the main dining room for breakfast before leaving on their journey up the St. Lawrence River.

As they were having their breakfast, the Governor informed them that he had made arrangements with several Algonquians to paddle their canoes and act as protectors on their journey.

Immediately after breakfast, the group was led down the path to the shoreline where the Algonquians and canoes were waiting. Dollard and the nun were assigned into one canoe and the Jesuits in another. The governor wished them Godspeed. The canoes pushed off and began their journey up the river.

Dollard was seated next to the young nun and he had a harquebus in his hands at the ready. After about a mile, he asked the young nun, "Excuse me, Soeur, we have traveled from France together, but we have not been formally introduced. I am Adam Dollard and may I ask your name?"

The young nun seemed uneasy speaking with this handsome young Frenchman, but she aroused her courage and said, "My name is Soeur Adelaise."

"Is that your birth name, or is that the name given to you when you took your final vows?" he inquired.

"It's my birth name. When I take my final vows, I will take the name of a saint," she responded.

"Then you're a novitiate?" he inquired

"Yes," she said.

Dollard took a slight pause. "Does that mean that if you decide you don't want to remain in the religious life you may leave?"

"Yes, that's what it means," she responded looking straight ahead.

Dollard could tell from her curt response that she didn't want to continue the conversation. He sat quietly and observed the shoreline for any Iroquoian activity. He had been warned by the governor that the Iroquois were everywhere in the forest around Quebec.

The trip from Quebec to Trois-Rivieres was about eighty miles against the current. Dollard asked one of the Algonquians who spoke French how long it took by canoe to reach their first destination. He was told it took two full days. Furthermore, they expected to remain at Trois-Rivieres for a day while they picked up some supplies to take to Ville-Marie (Montreal). The Algonquian told him that once they reached Ville-Marie, the Jesuits and he planned to rest for a few days before continuing up the St. Lawrence and the Ottawa to the Huron missions. "This will be another journey of several hundred more miles," the Native American pointed out.

The Algonquians stopped every three hours to rest and hydrate themselves. That gave everyone in the canoes a chance to stretch their legs and speak with the passengers in the other canoes. Dollard attempted to engage Soeur Adelaise in conversation, but he was unsuccessful.

A few of the Algonquians were curious about Soeur Adelaise,

and when they had an opportunity, they would brush up against her at several of their stops. This close contact with these Native Americans had her very uneasy. Dollard began to notice the Algonquians fascination with this young nun, so he decided to move in and protect her. He took her by the arm and marched her off from the main group. Dollard let the Algonquians know by his posture that Soeur Adelaise was his property and she was off limits. The natives discontinued their aggression.

They paddled another twenty-five miles when they once again stopped for a respite. The Jesuits would use this opportunity to say their "Office of Readings" which they were required to say, daily. The Algonquians sometimes would be loud and boisterous; this would distract the Jesuits from their concentration. At this stop, Pere Brebeuf decided to step into the forest to concentrate on his required prayers. After about a half hour, when the group was about to depart, Dollard walked to the edge of the forests and began to call for Pere Brebeuf. There was no answer. He stepped into the forest and there wasn't any sign of him.

About a half-hour prior, Brebeuf had opened his prayer book just after he stepped into the forest. He looked ahead to ensure that he wouldn't walk into a tree; he spotted an open area in the heavily forested surroundings, and began to traverse through the trees. He began to say his Office as he cautiously walked along. The prayers of the Office usually would take about forty-five minutes to read from beginning to the end.

Brebeuf was very religious and disciplined since childhood, and he had an ability to block out any surroundings, especially when he was praying. As he was concluding his reading, he decided it was time to retrace his steps and head back to the river. It was at that exact moment when he realized that he wasn't sure which direction he should take to reach his destination. At that point, he made a fatal mistake and began to walk in the wrong direction.

When it was learned among the group that Brebeuf was missing, the Algonquians became very agitated. They were in heavily traveled Iroquois territory, and if this group were to be discovered by one of their war parties, it could prove to be fatal.

Dollard, the other Jesuits, and Soeur Adelaise wanted the Algonquians to go into the forest and search for him. The leader of that Native American group flatly refused. They did agree, however, not to continue the journey immediately, and to wait a reasonable amount of time to see if he would emerge from the forest.

Deep in the forest, Brebeuf began to panic. He knew that he was in trouble and had no idea which direction the river was located. It began to get dark so he decided to sit down by a tree and prayed to God to point him in the right direction. Since he was completely exhausted, he fell asleep.

Back at the river, the Algonquians compromised and agreed to wait until the morning before continuing their journey. If Brebeuf hadn't returned by then, the guides were going to leave and assume that the priest would never be found.

Two hours after sunrise, Dollard, Pere Lalemant and Soeur Adelaise pleaded with the Algonquians not to proceed, but their pleas fell on deaf ears. The Algonquian leader, Red Fox, stated that if they didn't get into the canoe, he would leave them on the beach.

Dollard escorted the young nun into the canoe and the whole party shoved off. It was at that point that the group was about twenty-miles from Trois-Rivieres.

On the second day of being lost in this immense forest, Brebeuf decided to continue walking with the hope that he would eventually find the river and his companions. He walked all day, but all he managed to do was to drift farther into the forest. Once again as night fell, he sat down by a tree and fell into another deep sleep.

When Brebeuf awakened in the morning, he was beginning to show signs of dehydration. It had been nearly three days since he had water or sustenance. He stood reluctantly and stumbled along. After an hour of aimlessly wandering about, he heard footsteps coming in his direction. Through the trees he saw a group of natives heading in his direction. He ran to the leader and embraced him. The startled native moved him to arm's length, and handed him his canteen as he could see his was on the verge of dehydration. Once Brebeuf was hydrated, he explained through sign language to the native leader that he was in search of the river. The leader gave a sign for him to follow the group. After two hours of walking, and about twenty-five feet from the river's edge, the Algonquians uncovered from the brush their hidden canoes, dragged them to the river and launched them.

Brebeuf bargained with this hunting party to take him to Trois-Rivieres so he could reunite with his original group. This particular group had been hunting beaver fur and they were anxious to get down to Quebec to trade.

Brebeuf told them through sign language that if they would take him up river, he would ensure that they would get at least or maybe more for their furs at Trois-Rivieres. He also assured them that the church at the trading post would give them a reward for bringing him to them. Eventually, they agreed.

Dollard and his group reached Trois-Rivieres late the next day. When the two Jesuits that were assigned to the trading post learned of Pere Brebeuf's loss, they spent the next few hours deciding which one of them would take his place and go to the mission with Lalemant in the north. It was finally agreed that Pere Giraud, since he was the youngest and hardier, would make the trip to the Huron mission and relieve Pere Jabari who had been serving there for three years.

Soeur Adelaise, immediately upon arrival, took up her position at the makeshift hospital. Dollard spent the few hours they intended to be at Trois-Rivieres speaking with the men and getting as much information as possible about Ville-Marie.

Early the next morning, and just as they were about to leave, the group of Algonquians that were transporting Pere Brebeuf arrived at Trois-Rivieres. Everyone greeted him as if he had arisen from the dead. Dollard convinced their Algonquian party to stay over another day at the trading post to allow Pere Brebeuf time to rest.

The person happiest to see Pere Brebeuf was Pere Giraud. Now he wouldn't have to take that dangerous trip north and be subjected to being captured by the Iroquois. The next leg of the trip was a little over a hundred miles, and this time of the year, the Iroquois were vigilant. The five nations had committed to erasing the French from the island of Ville-Marie. The island had once been the site of an Iroquois settlement over a hundred years before and they considered the land sacred.

Just as the day was breaking, the Algonquians, Dollard, Peres Brebeuf and Lalemant began their trek up the St. Lawrence. As they did on the first leg of the trip, they would stop every three hours to rest and hydrate. Pere Brebeuf had learned his lesson the hard way and he remained with the group when they would make these temporary stops.

At the end of the third day, they finally arrived at Ville-Marie. One of the Algonquian had paddled ahead to announce their arrival. This gave the governor, Paul de Chomedey de

Maisonneuve, advanced notice, and he came down to the dock to greet Peres Brebeuf, Lalemant, and Dollard.

As Dollard stepped ashore, de Chomedey shook his hand and welcomed him to their little settlement. "We have much to talk about, Monsieur Dollard. I have heard a lot of good things about you from Jean de Lauson. I am looking forward to having you make a contribution to the little community of Ville-Marie.

"Thank you, Excellency, and I thank you for the opportunity."

The governor slowly walked him to his house where a lunch was being prepared in his honor. Pere Brebeuf had previously met the governor when he had returned from a three-year stay at the Huron mission six years ago. Brebeuf and Lalemant stayed for lunch, but they had decided to skip dinner, since they were anxious to leave for their northern mission at first light.

Ville-Marie was a fortress that protected the French traders from the Iroquois. It was laid out in the typical fortress design of the 17th century with four bastions protruding out to cover the inter walls. All around the entire fortress walls was an eight foot walkway with cannon every hundred feet. Each of the bastions had a sentinel stationed within its confines. There were three gates that allowed the farmers ingress and egress to their fields. The interior rows of small houses that were surrounded by an open area that was to be used as a parade field when the militia was eventually formed. The gate facing the St. Lawrence River had attached to it a pier that extended into the river, and was used to dock visiting boats and allowed loading and unloading of goods. It was common knowledge that the island was infested with Iroquois bent on ambushing and killing French farmers working in their fields.

The governor's house was by far the largest dwelling within the fort. When they arrived at the governor's house, Dollard was greeted by the governor's daughter, an eighteen-year-old woman by the name of Bernadette. Although he was immediately struck with her youth and beauty, he was decidedly cautious. It was this kind of situation that had got him into trouble with the authorities and the military back in France. He didn't want to revisit a similar situation.

After a seven course dinner, the governor and Adam retired to another room where the situation at Ville-Marie was explained in detail.

"I requested from the governor of Quebec to send someone with a military background, such as yours, to train our men. We are under constant threat from the Iroquois. Our little colony is limited to this fortress and the few plowed fields that are adjacent to its walls. These fields are constantly under attack from these devils. They appear, kill a farmer, and disappear as quickly as they appeared. We have to provide an armed guard to walk along with the farmer while he plows the field, but on several occasions, the armed guard and the farmer are both attacked and killed," he explained as he lit his pipe.

He continued, "Tomorrow morning, I will introduce you to the male population of the fort as the garrison commander. I would like you to immediately begin a military training program and to educate our male population in the art of making war. Evicting the Iroquois from this island should be the number one priority."

Dollard took a slight pause and then he said, "I will study this problem and begin immediately on establishing a militia. I assume that I will be given a free hand in taking whatever action is necessary to accomplish this mission?"

"You, sir, will be given all the support that I can muster. This little army will be directly under your command," the governor responded.

After they drank another two bottles of wine, Adam was shown to his temporary quarters in the governor's mansion.

Early the next morning and after the morning meal, Adam was introduced to one Charles Le Moyne who had spent the last year attempting to put together a group of armed men to rid the island of the infestation of Iroquois. Le Moyne spent the rest of the day taking Adam from house to house introducing him to the Ville-Marie men. The governor posted a proclamation requiring all men, sixteen years of age and older, to report to Adam in the open area in front of the rows of small houses for military instruction and drill first thing in the morning.

The men didn't resist this order from the governor. They were well aware that the Iroquois were the scourge of all New France.

That afternoon when Adam returned to the governor's residence, one of his servants took him to a small house within the fort that had been constructed in anticipation of his arrival. It had two large rooms. It was located on the St. Lawrence River side of the fortress, just behind one of the walls that protected the city. It was furnished with a bed, dining table, chairs, and a clothing rack for the few clothes he had in his possession. In the middle of the dining table was a vase with a bouquet of roses and a note:

"I am so glad that you were able to come here and assist our men in protecting this little colony. I look forward to becoming your friend.

Warmly,

Bernadette."

Adam smiled as he thought briefly of his time with Geruese and how that had changed his life.

He began to organize his little house while placing his personal things around and hanging up the few clothes he owned. He had brought several bottles of wine from Quebec, took them out of his pack and placed them in the corner of the room. He selected one bottle, opened it, and poured a glass as he began to contemplate the military program that he was sent there to establish.

Just as he completed drinking the glass of wine, a light tapping on his door broke his concentration. He walked to the door and opened it. Standing before him were two Ursuline's nuns.

Adam extended his hand as he said, "Good day, Soeurs, may I be of some assistance? My name is Adam Dollard."

"We know who you are, Monsieur Dollard. May we come in?" Soeur Marie inquired.

Adam stepped aside and allowed them to enter his humble little house. "Please, Soeurs, please sit down."

They each sat on one of the three chairs that were available. Adam sat down facing them. "What may I do for you, Soeurs?" he inquired.

"Let me introduce ourselves, my name is Soeur Marie, and this is Soeur Adair. We live in the Ursuline's Convent within the walled city. We have heard so much about you. This colony needs your military experience. We are under threat from the Iroquois continually. They are everywhere and nowhere. They ambush the farmers in the field so silently that we don't learn that the poor man is dead until he doesn't arrive home to his family at the end of the day."

Soeur Marie took a short pause and then she said, "Soeur Adair and I made a large kettle of stew and it's much more than the two of us can eat. We would be honored if you would come by the Convent this evening and have a bowl with us?"

As he looked at these two young nuns, he wondered what brought them to this wilderness where there is death all around. *These ladies are being neighborly and I can't refuse their invitation,* he thought.

"I would be delighted to accept your supper invitation, Soeurs. Quite frankly, I wasn't sure what I was going to do for dinner tonight. I haven't had time to stock in provisions. Your patron saint must have sent you to rescue me," he said with jest.

The nuns smiled and stood to leave. "Our Convent is a block down the street. There is a sign just outside the building. We are also trained nurses and the Convent serves as a hospital as well. We'll expect you around five o'clock," Soeur Marie said. They disappeared through the doorway and Adam closed the door behind them.

Adam sat back down with pen and paper and began to draft a lesson plan for the training of a French soldier. He was familiar with training new troops in France while he served as a lieutenant and overseeing the platoon of regulars in Paris that guarded the King. He knew that the first thing a soldier must learn to do was March. Marching teaches the soldier to take commands without question. After the soldier is conditioned to taking and responding to orders without question, the rest of the discipline process just falls into place.

He worked on this outline for a few hours until it was time to walk down to the Convent and have dinner with the nuns.

As he walked down St. Paul Street toward the Convent, he noticed every thirty or so feet along the wall that protected the city from invasion was a young Frenchman, harquebus in hand, ensuring that an Iroquois did not slip through during the night. He knew that his first order of business would be ridding the island of these devils that terrorized the population of Ville-Marie.

When he arrived at the Convent, he rang the exterior bell that hung along the outside door. Within seconds, Soeur Marie opened the heavy wooden door.

"Welcome to our modest Convent, Monsieur." She stood aside and allowed Adam entrance.

There were a few windows and a heavy smell of incense. Religious pictures lined the walls as he walked through the first room and into a second. A table was set for three and a flower arrangement was in the middle surrounded by place settings.

"Please sit down. Would you like a glass of wine?" she asked.

"Yes, please," he responded.

Soeur Adair retrieved the wine from a cabinet and handed the bottle to Adam. "If you would be so kind as to open the bottle," she handed him a corkscrew. "I brought this bottle from Paris. It was given to me by my father before I left for New France," she said with a smile.

"Do you miss Paris, Soeur Adair?" he inquired.

As he sat down next to Soeur Marie she said, "I miss my family, yes, although, I didn't see them frequently while I was in Paris. My parents were allowed to visit with me every six months until I took my final vows. Shortly thereafter, I was told that I would be coming to New France and serve the French people here. That was two years ago."

Soeur Marie spoke next, "We are so grateful that you are here, Monsieur. The men at this outpost are trappers and farmers, not soldiers like you. The Iroquois are warriors and are trained in the art of forest warfare. Our men desperately need the training that you can provide to them as an insurance that this settlement will survive."

The large pot of stew was in the center of the table. Soeur Marie began to dish out the stew starting with Adam and large piece of freshly baked bread was given to him as well.

They questioned him throughout the dinner about his background. He told them about attending the military school in Paris and his experience in the army, but didn't provide any specific details. The governor had previously shared with the community information concerning Adam's resume, and everyone was confident he would be the right person to indoctrinate the men of the Ville-Marie to protect them from the Iroquois.

After the dinner and conversation with the nuns, Soeur Adair insisted that he take with him the half full bottle of wine for another day. He thanked the Soeurs and walked back to his quarters.

At dawn the next morning, he fixed some coffee that had been provided to him by Bernadette when she arranged his living quarters. Then he left for the little parade field in the center of the town. Several of the town men were already there waiting for him. Within a few minutes, about thirty young men between the ages of sixteen and thirty were formed up in columns of four with the tallest of the men in the front ranks

Adam began his instruction, "Men, the first thing we have to agree upon is to recognize that the enemy of this little army is the Iroquois. They are formable in numbers. They were born and raised in these forests and know this land better than any one of us. I come from a military tradition where an army meets its enemy on an open battlefield. Here, in this land, the enemy is hiding in the forest and attacks you when you are the most vulnerable. We must learn from them. The one thing I want you to understand is that we will fight as a unit. The Iroquois, from what I've been told, fight as individuals. I've also been told that they have little patience for a siege. In other words, they have a short attention span. That is where they are vulnerable. We will take advantage of their shortcomings and kill them at every turn. The first thing I want you to learn is how to march. This will teach you discipline and how to work together as a unit. If we fight as a unit, a few of us will kill many of them. Once you learn these skills, we will take this island back, and the farmers will be able to farm without looking over their shoulder a hundred times a day. Now I want you to lead off with your left foot and begin to move forward. When I say halt, I want you to stop immediately. Ready, march," he commanded.

He spent most of the morning teaching them to move forward and stop at his command. In the afternoon, he taught them to turn left, right, and about face as one unit.

Near the end of the day, Le Moyne came down to the parade field to observe the men training. He watched intently, and at one point he offered a suggestion. Adam turned to him and said, "Sir, too many cooks spoil the broth," and he continued barking commands. Le Moyne took the hint and left the parade field.

That evening when he returned to his quarters, he found Bernadette sitting at his table with a basket of dinner that she had prepared for him. He was somewhat surprised. "What are you doing here, Mademoiselle?" he inquired.

"Father had the cook prepare you a dinner. I volunteered to bring it to you," she coyly said.

"That is very thoughtful of both you and your father. Would you like to sit and talk with me while I devour this wonderful food," he said.

"I would love to sit and talk with you. I don't have much opportunity to converse with someone as cultured and educated as you. The majority of men at this settlement are either fur traders or farmers with little or no formal education," she emphasized.

"And where were you educated may I ask?" he inquired as he opened the basket of food on the table.

"I was born in Paris, but my parents brought me to New France before I was a year old. My father came here to build the fort while my mother and I remained in Quebec. I was sent to the Convent School operated by the Ursuline nuns, and then last year I came here. Now I'm locked away in a fort, where the majority of residents cannot read or write." She observed Adam studying the food. "Please, serve yourself and eat, I had my dinner before coming here."

Adam removed the baked duck, salad, and freshly baked rolls from the basket and put it carefully on a plate. Also in the basket is a bottle of French wine. He opened the bottle, poured two glasses, and offered the second glass to Bernadette.

Bernadette took a sip of the wine and then she said, "Father believes that you will be able to remove the Iroquois from the island. He says that your formal military background is exactly what this fort needs. Our Huron friends were intimidated by the Iroquois and they deserted us about two months ago. They went down the St. Lawrence to Quebec where they believe it's safer."

As Adam ate his dinner, he took a drink of wine. "Until now, the Iroquois were a chapter in a book that I read while studying military tactics at the university. I remember thinking they would be an easy enemy to defeat. Their modus operandi is all based on their ability to blend into the terrain and employ an element of surprise on their enemy. From what I understand from the men that I was training today, the Iroquois will lay in wait for a day or two, and then sneak up on the unsuspecting farmer, killing him instantly."

"Yes, they have killed two farmers within the past month. When the farmer doesn't come home at the end of the day, the men form a search party. They usually find his mutilated body in a field," she said with a touch of fright in her voice.

"As soon as I can get the men tactically trained, we will sweep across this island and remove every Iroquois invader," he promised.

"We haven't had a shipment of fur from up north in over a year. The Iroquois lay in wait for either the Huron or our French traders to come down one of the rivers and attack them. I have been told that they take the furs they steal down to Fort Orange and trade them to the Dutch who have a settlement there," she told him.

Bernadette took another sip of her wine, and then she said, "So what are your future plans? Do you intend to settle here at Ville-Marie, or will you become like most of the men who come up this river and become a fur trapper?"

"I don't know anything about fur trapping. I am a soldier. I will command a small army to defeat the Iroquois and protect the New France settlers." Adam took a pause from eating his meal. "And what does the future hold for you?"

"I intend to stay here until spring, and then I will return to Quebec to assist the nuns teaching at the school. Eventually, I would like to go to France and stay with my relatives there. Who knows, maybe I will be introduced to a nice young man and become a wife," she said with a voice of confidence.

Adam took a drink of his wine, but he wanted to be careful with his next words. "Please don't think that I am being familiar, but you are a very attractive, educated young woman that many men I am acquainted with in France would surely want to court under the proper circumstance. Believe me: you won't have any trouble finding someone to ask for your hand."

"You're very kind and flattering, sir, but now I must get home or my father will begin to question my absence."

They stood from the table and he escorted her to the door.

"Goodnight and I thank you and your father for being such good hosts."

She turned to him and kissed him on the cheek. "Goodnight, sir and we all look forward to having you serve and protect us in this little fortress of Ville-Marie." As she left, he watched her cross the parade field and enter the governor's house.

He closed the door and crossed to the table. He poured another glass of wine and thought to himself, *I have to keep focused. Mademoiselle Bernadette is a very beautiful and educated young woman. It would be easy for her to take my mind off of my mission here.*

Four

*O*n the 2nd of June, 1658, the ship St. Andre laid in the harbor of Rochelle, crowded with passengers for New France. She had served two years as a hospital for marines, and was infected with a contagious fever. Including the crew, some two hundred additional persons were on board, more than half of who were bound for Ville-Marie.

Most of these were sturdy laborers, artisans, peasants, and soldiers, together with a troop of young women to be presented to the men of New France for the possibility of marriage—a portion of the company set down on the old record as "sixty virtuous men and thirty-two pious girls." There were two Jesuits as well, Guillaume de Vignal and Padraig Le Maltre, both destined to a speedy death at the hands of the Iroquois.

But the most conspicuous among these passengers for Ville-Marie were two groups of women in the habit of nuns, under the direction of Marguerite Bourgeoys and Jeanne Mance.

Marguerite Bourgeoys, whose kind, womanly face bespoke her fitness for the task, was founder of the school for female children at Ville-Marie; her companion, a tall, austere figure, worn with suffering and care, was directress of the hospital. Both of these women had returned to France for aid, and were now on their way back to New France, each with three recruits, three being a mystic number, as a type of the Holy Family, to whose worship they were especially devoted.

Amid the bustle of departure, the shouts of sailors, the rattling of cordage, the flapping of sails, the tears and the embracing, an elderly man with heavy plebeian features, sallow with disease, and in a sober, half-clerical dress, approached Mademoiselle Mance and her three nuns, and, turning his eyes to heaven, spread his hands over them in benediction. It was Le Royer de la Dauversiere, founder of the sisterhood of St. Joseph, to which the three nuns belonged. "Now, O Lord," he exclaimed, with the look whose mission on earth fulfilled, "permit thou thy servants to depart in peace!"

Soeur Maillet, who had charge of the meager treasury of the community, thought that something more than a blessing was due from him and asked where she should apply for payment of the interest of the twenty-thousand livres which Mademoiselle Mance had given him, to invest.

Dauversiere changed his demeanor, and replied, with a troubled voice, "My daughter, God will provide for you. Place your trust in Him." He was bankrupt, and had used the money of the sisterhood to pay a debt of his own, leaving the nuns penniless.

Many people in France found it amazing how an association of devotees, inspired, as they supposed from heaven, had undertaken to found a religious colony at Ville-Marie in honor of the Holy Family. The essentials of the proposed establishment were to be a seminary of Jesuits dedicated to the Virgin, a hospital to Saint Joseph, and a school to the Infant Jesus while a settlement was to be formed around them simply for their defense and maintenance.

It was seventeen years since Mademoiselle Mance had begun her labors in honor of Saint Joseph. Marguerite Bourgeoys had entered upon hers more recently; yet even then the attempt was premature, for she found no white children to teach.

In time, however, this want was supplied, and she opened her school in a stable, which answered to the stable of Bethlehem, lodging with her pupils in the loft, and instructing them in Roman Catholic Christianity, with such rudiments of mundane knowledge as she and her advisors thought fit to impart.

Mademoiselle Mance found no lack of hospital work, for blood and blows were rife at Ville-Marie, where the woods were full of Iroquois, and not a moment was without its peril.

Though the years began to tell upon her, she toiled patiently at her dreary task, till, in January of 1657, she fell on the ice of the St. Lawrence, broke her right arm, and dislocated the left wrist. Bonchard, the surgeon at Ville-Marie, set the broken bones, but did not discover the dislocation of the wrist. As a result of this oversight, the arm in consequence became totally useless, and her health wasted away under incessant and violent pain.

Maisonneuve, the governor of the settlement, advised her to go to France for treatment. Marguerite Bourgeoys, whose pupils, white and red, had greatly multiplied, resolved to go with her. They set out in July, 1657, landed in Rochelle, and went directly to Paris. They were received at the seminary of St. Sulpice, for the Jesuits of this community were joined with them in the work at Ville-Marie, of which they were afterwards to become the feudal proprietors.

It is said that a wonderful event ensued, if we may trust the evidence. Olier, the founder of St. Sulpice, had lately died, and the two pilgrims would pay homage to his heart, which the Jesuits of his community kept as a precious relic, enclosed in a leaden box. The box was brought when the thought inspired Mademoiselle Mance to try its miraculous reputation and invoke the intercession of the departed founder. She did so, touching her disabled arm gently with the leaden casket. Instantly, grateful warmth pervaded the shriveled limb, and from that hour its use was restored.

It is true that the Jesuits ventured to doubt the Sulpitian miracle and even ridiculed it, but the Sulpitians will show to this day the attestation of Mademoiselle Mance herself, written with the fingers once paralyzed and powerless. Nevertheless, the cure was not so thorough as to permit her again to treat her patients.

Her main purpose for being in France was to visit Madame de Bullion, a devout lady of great wealth, who was usually designated at Ville-Marie as "the unknown benefactress," because, though her charities were the mainstay of the Ville-Marie colony, and though the source from which they proceeded was well known, she affected, in the interest of humility, the greatest secrecy, and required those who profited by her gifts to pretend ignorance from their source.

Overflowing with a zeal for the pious enterprise at Ville-Marie, she received Mademoiselle Mance with enthusiasm and lent an open ear to her presentation. After a half-hour and two cups of tea, she paid over to her a large sum of money that exceeded twenty-two thousand francs.

With her acquired funding, she departed for the town of La Fleche to visit Le Royer de la Dauversiere. He was a fanatic, who, through visions and revelations, had first conceived the plan of a hospital in honor of Saint Joseph at Ville-Marie. He had found in Mademoiselle Mance a zealous and efficient pioneer, but the execution of his scheme required a community of hospital nuns, and therefore he had labored for the last eighteen years to form one at La Fleche and was planning to send nuns in due time to New France.

Dauversiere believed that the time had now arrived. He chose three nuns for the journey. They were Soeurs Bresoles, Mace, and Maillet. They were sent under escort of certain pious gentlemen to Rochelle to board the ship. However, their exit from La Fleche was not without difficulties. Dauversiere had a bad reputation pertaining to his handling of financial dealings, and because at various times he inspired virtuous girls from La Fleche with religious excitement and shipping them to the New World against the will of their parents. It was rumored through the town that Dauversiere kidnapped and sold them. The rumor continued that he was luring away three young nuns. A mob gathered at the Convent gates, and the escort was forced to draw their swords to open the way for the terrified Soeurs.

Of the twenty-two thousand francs which she had received, Mademoiselle Mance kept two thousand for immediate needs, and gave the remainder to Dauversiere who had been pressed by his creditors. He was sick at the time with the gout and was in a depressed state.

One of the miracles in the early annals of Ville-Marie was considering his condition at the time. Nevertheless, he was able to go to Rochelle and bid farewell to the nuns. When he finally returned home, he was overcome with a host of maladies and died a lingering and painful death.

While Mademoiselle Mance was gaining recruits in La Fleche, Marguerite Bourgeoys was also successful in her native town of Troyes, and she eventually rejoined her companions at Rochelle. She was accompanied by Soeurs Chatel, Crolo, and Raisin, her assistants at the school in Ville-Marie.

Meanwhile, the Sulpitians and others interested in the pious enterprise in New France had spared no effort to gather men to strengthen the colony and young women to serve as their wives. Everyone was mustered at Rochelle, waiting for embarkation.

Their waiting was a long one.

Laval, the bishop at Quebec, was allied to the Jesuits and looked upon the colonists of Ville-Marie with more than coldness. His agents used every effort to discourage them, and that certain persons at Rochelle told the master of the ship in which the emigrants were to sail that they were not to be trusted to pay their passage. As a result, there was a delay of more than two months before means could be found to pay the prudent commander.

Finally, the company of missionaries crowded into a filthy and infected ship, were tossed for two months more on the relentless sea, buffeted by repeated storms and suffering from a contagious fever. The sickness attacked Mademoiselle Mance and she nearly succumbed. Eight or ten died on the trip over and their bodies were dropped into the sea after a prayer from the two Jesuits.

At last, a length of land was spotted and the piney odors of the forest were inhaled by this fragile little group as they sailed up the broad estuary of the St. Lawrence and anchored under the rock of Quebec.

High aloft on the edge of the cliff, they saw the fleur-de-lis waving above the fort of St. Louis, and beyond the cross on the tower of the cathedral silhouetted against the sky. The houses of the merchants were outlined on the stand below, and boats and canoes were drawn up along the bank.

When they reached the shoreline, they were greeted by the bishop and the Jesuits as co-workers in the holy cause of conversion. Though a unit against heresy, the pious founders of New France were far from a unity among themselves. To the thinking of the Jesuits, Ville-Marie was a government within a government, a wheel within a wheel. This rival Sulpitian settlement was in their eyes an element of disorganization adverse to the disciplined harmony of the Church of New France with its focus at Quebec.

Now that all difficulties had been overcome, the entire group from France, with the exception of the three young nuns who were too sick to make the journey up the St. Lawrence, embarked on boats and ascended the St. Lawrence, leaving Quebec infected with the contagion they had brought from France. The journey that can now be made in a single night cost them fifteen days of hardship and danger.

At length they reached their new home. Ville-Marie lay before them, still gasping between life and death, in a puny, precarious infancy. Some forty small, compact houses were ranged parallel to the river, along a line of what is now St. Paul Street. On the left, there was a fort, and on a rising ground at the right a massive windmill of stone, enclosed with a wall pierced for harquebus, and answering the purpose of a redoubt or blockhouse. There were fields studded with charred and blackened stumps, between which crops were growing and stretched away to the edges of the bordering forest, and the green, shaggy back of the mountain towered over them.

There were, at this time, a hundred and sixty men at Ville-Marie, about fifty of whom had families, or at least wives. They greeted the newcomers with a welcome, which, this time, was as sincere as it was warm, and bestirred them with alacrity to provide them with shelter for the winter. After the first winter, the newcomers managed to pay for lodging to be built with the funds that Mademoiselle Mance had obtained before they left France. Once their housing was built they were occupied for many years. The houses were hastily built of ill-seasoned planks that allowed the piercing cold of the New France winter through countless cracks and chinks, and driving snow sifted through in such quantities that they were sometimes obliged, the morning after a storm, to remove it with shovels. Their food would freeze on the table before them, and the coarse brown bread had to be thawed on the hearth before they could cut it.

Since there was not enough room within the palisade to build a hospital, it was constructed on the periphery of the fort and therefore was exposed. The Iroquois would skulk at night around the building like wolves in a camp of sleeping travelers on the prairies, though the human foe was bolder, fiercer, and more bloodthirsty. More than once one of these prowling warriors was known to have crouched all night in a rank growth of wild mustard in the garden of the nuns, vainly hoping that one of them would come within reach of his tomahawk.

During the summer, a month rarely passed without confrontation with the Iroquois, resulting in a clatter of harquebus and adding to the list of patients in the hospital. It was about this time when the governor of Ville-Marie sent a letter to the governor of Quebec requesting he send someone who had professional military experience in France. It was about that time that Adam Dollard arrived.

At the end of the summer in 1658, the three nuns, Soeurs Bresoles, Mace, and Maillet had recovered from the disease they had carried from France. It was finally decided to send them to Ville-Marie. Adam Dollard had left for Ville-Marie in the spring and it was reported that he had arrived there safely to assume his duties as commander of the little settlement.

They were put into two canoes under the care of Francois Hertel and four Algonquians. Although the three nuns were wished farewell by the bishop and the Jesuits of Quebec, they were hoping that they would never reach their destination, Ville-Marie. They would have liked to have nuns from the Hotel Dieu of Quebec, who would be under their control. Thus was the division that existed among these Catholic Orders during the early days of New France.

When the canoes with the nuns aboard began to paddle up the St. Lawrence, the eyes of the Iroquois were upon them. The Iroquois had scouts that surrounded the city of Quebec at that time.

About five miles from their point of departure, three Iroquois canoes with six warriors in each began a pursuit. In no time they began to move in rapidly. The Algonquians who were paddling the nuns canoes, guided them toward the shoreline, leaped out of the craft, and disappeared into the forest.

The young nuns remained in the canoes and were overcome with fear as the Iroquois paddled toward them. Francois Hertel took hold of his harquebus, climbed out of the canoe, leveled it at the nearest Iroquois canoe, and fired. He scored a direct hit on the warrior sitting in front of the first craft. Francois began to load his weapon again when the second canoe of Iroquois beached. Two of them jumped out and within seconds were on him. One of them took his stone tomahawk and struck him in the head. Francois fell to the ground unconscious. The warriors tied his hands behind his back and loaded him into the canoe that held the single nun. Four Iroquois took control of the French canoes, two in each. They set a course for the Richelieu River.

When they reached the mouth of the river, they beached their canoes and tied Francois to a tree; the nuns were hastily pulled from the canoes and stripped of their habits and outer garments. The Iroquois built a fire and camped for the night. Francois expected to be tortured, but that would come later. All of the prisoners were fed and given blankets for the night, except Francois.

Early the next morning the prisoners were again loaded into

the canoes and the Iroquois paddled down the Richelieu until it emptied into Lake Champlain. They camped that night on an island in the middle of the lake. In the morning, they continued their journey down the lake until they reached its head. There, they camped on the portage between Lake Champlain and Lake George.

At first light, they began their trip forty miles down Lake George and arrived at its end by late evening. They were in a hurry to get to their village which was situated a few miles up the river Mohawk. They were finally required to stop around 8:00 P.M. when the sun finally set. They were still two days from their destination.

In the morning, another party of Iroquois came into their camp. Their destination was an island in the Richelieu where six hundred Iroquois warriors were gathering for an attack on Quebec. The party with the nuns and Francois began to move at a fast pace toward their destination.

After another day of double time travel, they reached the river Mohawk. Canoes had been left on the beach by the war party that they had met two days hence. Everyone was loaded into the canoes and these Iroquois warriors began a fast paddling pace up the river.

By noon time, the Mohawk village came into view. It was located on a hill overlooking the river. The canoes were beached and one of the warriors ran ahead to inform the villagers to be prepared to greet the prisoners. By greeting the prisoners, the Mohawk would make the male prisoner run the gauntlet. About fifty percent of those who were required to run the gauntlet never made it to the end and were beaten to death. Fortunately, for Francois, the majority of the warriors had left to join the army of Iroquois at the Richelieu. The two lines that were formed were made up of women and old men. Francois stood a good chance to reach the end of the line. However, this didn't mean he would escape torture.

After Francois successfully ran the gauntlet, he was tied to a stake in the middle of the village and children threw stones at him. He was stripped of his clothes and the women began to beat him with branches with thorns at the end. It wasn't long before he was a mass of blood. Having sufficiently amused themselves, they left him in peace for a while. Several minutes later, an old one-eyed Indian approached, walked around in back of the stake where he was bound, and took his hands and examined them. He selected the left forefinger and then he called to a child about four or five years of age, handed him a knife, and told him to cut off the finger.

After this preliminary torture, Francois would have been burned to death had not a squaw happily adopted him in place of her deceased brother. He was untied and installed at once in the lodge of his new relatives. He was required to put on leggings, moccasins, and greasy shirt.

The nuns were divided up among the woman of the village for use at hard labor. One of the nuns, Soeur Bresoles, who had defied her parents and ran away to join the religious order, caught the eye of one her Mohawk captives. He demanded that she be turned over to him as a concubine. He took her to his lodge, stripped her down, and took her virginity.

A month later, the Mohawks agreed to a temporary peace with the French. One of the conditions was that all prisoners on both sides would be returned. Soeur Bresoles had settled into her life with her Mohawk warrior and they had married. She was also pregnant. She wrote a letter to Mademoiselle Mance explaining that she was in love with her Mohawk husband and she carried his child. Therefore, she decided to remain with him at the Mohawk village. She asked the Mademoiselle to write her parents a letter, explain her situation, and to tell them that she was happy in her new chosen life. Her letter was carried to Quebec by the freed prisoners.

The truce between the French and the Iroquois only lasted a few weeks. Three or four Iroquois came to Ville-Marie while Nicolas Gode and Jean Saint-Pere were on the roof of their house laying thatch. One of the warriors, armed with a harquebus, aimed it at Saint-Pere and fired. The man fell to the ground dead. They proceeded to cut off his head and carry it to their village. This, and several other incidents in New France, brought this weak truce to a climax.

In November 1658, a priest by the name of Guillaume de Vignal, who had recently arrived at Ville-Marie, went with thirteen men in a flatboat and several canoes to the Isle a la Pierre, nearly opposite Ville-Marie, to get stone for the seminary, which the priest had recently begun to build. With him was a thirty-year-old valiant gentleman named Claude de Brigeac, who had come as a soldier to Ville-Marie in the hope of dying in the defense of the true church and reaping the reward of a martyr.

Vignal, Claude de Brigeac and four men had scarcely landed when they were set upon by a large band of Iroquois who had been hiding among the bushes waiting to receive them. The rest of the French party, who were still in their boats upon seeing the Iroquois, retreated back to Ville-Marie.

Vignal was soon mortally wounded. Brigeac shot the chief dead with his harquebus, and then with pistol in hand, held the whole troop for an instant at bay, but his arm was shattered by a gunshot, and he was eventually seized, along with Vignal, Rene Cuillerier, and Jacques Dufresne.

Crossing to the main shore, immediately opposite Ville-Marie, the Iroquois made a small fort of logs and branches in which to shelter them and then began to dress the wounds of their prisoners. Upon seeing that Vignal was unable to make the journey to their villages, they killed him, divided his flesh, and roasted it for food.

Brigeac and his fellow prisoners spent a woeful night in this den of wolves, and in the morning their captors, having breakfasted on the remains of Vignal, began their homeward march dragging the Frenchmen with them.

Upon reaching Oneida, Brigeac was tortured to death with their customary atrocities. Cuillerier, who was present, reported that his tormentors could not wring from him a cry of pain, but throughout he continued to pray for their conversion. Cuillerier expected the same fate, but at the last minute an old squaw adopted him and saved his life. He eventually escaped his capturers, returned to Quebec by the circuitous, but comparatively safe route, of New Amsterdam and Boston.

In the following winter, Ville-Marie suffered an irreparable loss in the death of the brave Major Closse, a man whose intrepid coolness was never known to fail in the direst emergency. One day he went to the aid of a party of laborers attacked by the Iroquois. He was met by a crowd of warriors eager to kill or capture him. His servant who had accompanied him retreated leaving him alone to face the enemy. Closse snapped a pistol at the closest Iroquois, but it misfired. His remaining pistol misfired as well. Several Iroquois fired at him simultaneously and he was killed instantly.

The community of Ville-Marie eulogized him as "a brave soldier of Christ and the king." Some of his friends recalled him saying, "Messieurs, I came here only to die in the service of God;

and if I thought I could not die here, I would leave this country to fight Turks that I might not be deprived of such glory."

During the 1650s, the governor of Ville-Marie had erected redoubts of logs scattered about the outskirts of the settlement to serve as points of defense in case of attack while its citizens were farming their assigned areas. These redoubts bore the names of the saints, since it was believed that these little fortresses would offer more protection if they were under a higher protection.

The whole settlement was in a state of religious exaltation. The Iroquois were regarded as actual agents of Satan, and their warfare against Mary and her divine Son, those who died in fighting them, were held to merit the reward of martyrs, assured of a seat in paradise.

At the time, professional military assistance was lacking and the governor of Ville-Marie requested someone who could provide this desperately needed service. Adam Dollard had arrived from France and had the background that was required.

To paint a picture of the condition of New France at the time of Adam Dollard's arrival, the next several chapters, as recorded in the Jesuit Relations, will give the reader a short history of what these colonies were confronting.

Five

*T*here was an attack by the Iroquois at Trois Rivieres in 1658 that is worth mentioning. Until that time, the Huron's didn't dare go down to the French settlements, but out of desperation they resolved at all risks making the attempt. They were in need of kettles, hatchets, and knives that had become a necessity of life in their villages. Two hundred and fifty of their best warriors embarked under five valiant chiefs. They approached Trois Rivieres on the seventeenth of July, and, running their canoes ashore among the bulrushes, began to grease their hair, paint their faces, and otherwise adorn themselves that they might appear after a befitting fashion at the fort.

While they were thus engaged, an alarm was sounded. Some of the Huron warriors had discovered a large body of Iroquois, who had been for several days lurking in the forest unknown to the French garrison and watching for their opportunity to strike a blow.

The Huron's took up their weapons, and half greased and painted, ran to meet them. The Iroquois received them with a volley. The Huron's fell flat to avoid the shot, and then they leaped up with a furious yell, and sent back a shower of shots and arrows at the Iroquois. The Iroquois, who were outnumbered, gave way and fled with the exception of a few, who for a time countered the Huron's with their knives.

Eventually, the Huron's pursued and won the day. Many prisoners were taken, and many dead Iroquois were left on the field. The rout of the enemy was complete, and when their trading was ended, the Huron's returned home in triumph, decorated with the laurels and the scalps of victory. In the end, it would have been better for their families, and the missions, if they would have remained at home.

The Huron town of Teanaustaye, or St. Joseph, as referred to by the Jesuits, was located on the southeastern frontier of the Huron country. It was located near the foot of forest-covered hills and about fifteen miles from the settlement of Saint Marie. It had been the chief town of the Huron nation and its population by Huron standards was very large. The total population of the town was about four hundred families, and at least two thousand inhabitants. It was well fortified with palisades and was a solid bulwark in the Huron fashion. Here, countless of Iroquois had been burned and devoured over the years. Its people had been truculent and intractable heathen, but many of them had surrendered to the Roman Catholic faith under the preaching of Father Antoine Daniel.

On the morning of the fourth of July, when the forest around the village basked lazily in the early sun, one might have mounted the rising ground on which the town stood and passed un-challenged through the opening in the palisade. Within, one would have seen the crowded dwellings of bark, shaped like the arched coverings of huge baggage-wagons, decorated with the armorial devices of their owners and daubed on the outside with paint. Here some squalid wolfish dog lay sleeping in the sun, a group of Huron girls chattered together in the shade, an old squaw pounded corn in large wooden mortars, idle youth were gambling with cherry stones on a wooden platter, and naked infants crawled in the dust.

There was scarcely a warrior to be seen. Some were absent in quest of game or of Iroquois scalps, and some had gone with the trading party to the French settlements. If one were to follow the foul passageways among the houses, they would come to a church. The church was completely occupied since a mass had been conducted that morning. The participants were still kneeling in devotions.

Father Daniel had, the day before, returned to the village from a retreat at Saint Marie. Suddenly, voices shrilled with terror burst upon the silence of the town. The crowd was shouting, "The Iroquois! The Iroquois!" and the crowd continued screaming.

A large war party of hostile warriors had come in from the forest, and was rushing across the clearing toward the opening of the palisade.

Father Daniel ran out of the church and hurried toward these screaming warriors. Those who were capable grabbed their weapons to meet this menace head on; others rushed to and fro in the madness of blind panic. The priest rallied the defenders promising Heaven to those who defended their homes and their faith; then he hastened from house to house, calling on unbelievers to repent and receive baptism. They crowded around him, imploring to be saved. Daniel immersed his handkerchief into a bowl of water, shook it over them, and baptized them by aspersion.

The baptized Huron's pursued him as he ran again to the church, where he found a throng of women, children, and old men gathered as in a sanctuary. Some cried for baptism, some held out their children to receive it, some begged for absolution, and some wailed in terror and despair.

"Brothers," he exclaimed again and again, as he shook the baptismal drops from the handkerchief, "brothers, today we shall be in heaven."

The fierce yell of the war-whoop now rose close at hand. The palisade was forced open and the enemy was in the town. The air quivered with the infernal din. "Fly!" screamed the priest, driving his flock before him. "I will stay here. We shall meet again in Heaven."

Many of them escaped through an opening in the palisade opposite the side where the Iroquois was entering. Daniel did not follow. He wanted to give as many of his flock time to escape as possible. The hour had come for which he had long prepared himself.

In a moment, he saw the Iroquois and walked toward them from the church. When they saw him in turn, radiant in the vestments of his office, confronting them with a look kindled with the inspiration of martyrdom, they stopped and stared in amazement, then, recovering themselves, they bent their bows and showered him with a volley of arrows that tore through his robes and his flesh. A moment later, a gunshot followed that pierced his heart.

They rushed upon him with yells of triumph, stripped him naked, gashed and hacked his lifeless body, and scooping his blood in their hands, bathed their faces in it to make them look brave.

The town was in a blaze. When the flames reached the church, they flung the priest into it, and both were consumed together.

St. Joseph was a heap of ashes, and the victors took up their march with a train of nearly seven hundred prisoners, many of whom they killed along the way. Many more had been slain in the town and the neighboring forest, where the pursuers hunted them down, and where women, crouching for refuge among thickets, were betrayed by the cries and wailing of their infants.

The triumph of the Iroquois did not end here; for a neighboring fortified town, included within the circle of Daniel's mission, shared the fate of St. Joseph. Never had the Huron nation received such a blow.

More than eight months had passed since the catastrophe of St. Joseph. The winter was over and it was now spring. Around Saint Marie the forests were gray and bare, and, in the cornfields, the half-thawed soil, studded stalks of the last autumn harvest rose through the melting snow.

At nine o'clock on the morning of the sixteenth of March, the Jesuits saw a heavy smoke rising over the naked forest towards the southeast, three miles distant. They looked at each other in dismay. "The Iroquois, they are burning St. Louis!" one said to another. Flames mingled with the smoke; and, as they stood gazing, two Christian Huron's came breathless and aghast from the burning town. Their worst fear was realized. The Iroquois were there, but where were the Jesuits of the mission, Brebeuf and Lalemant?

Late in the autumn, a thousand Iroquois, chiefly Seneca's and Mohawks, had taken to the warpath for the Huron's. They had been all winter in the forest, hunting for subsistence and moving at their leisure towards their prey. The destruction of the two towns of the mission of St. Joseph had left a wide gap, and in the middle of March they entered the heart of the Huron country, undiscovered.

Common vigilance and common sense would have averted the calamities that followed, but the Huron's were like a doomed people, stupefied, sunk in dejection, fearing everything, yet taking no measures for defense. The Huron's could have met the invaders with double force, but the besotted warriors lay idle in their towns, or hunted at leisure in distant forests. The Jesuits could not rouse them to face the danger.

Before daylight on the sixteenth, the invaders approached St. Ignace, which with St. Louis and three other towns formed the mission of the same name. They reconnoitered the place in the darkness. It was defended on three sides by a deep ravine, and further strengthened by palisades fifteen or sixteen feet high. On the fourth side was protected by palisades alone, and these were left as usual, unguarded. This was not from a sense of security, for the greater part of the population had abandoned the town, believing it too much exposed to the enemy, and there remained only four hundred, chiefly women, children, and old men. The Huron warriors were absent hunting or on scalping-parties against the Iroquois.

It was just before dawn, when a yell startled the inhabitants from their sleep, and the Iroquois burst in upon them cutting them down with knives and hatchets, killing many and reserving the rest for a worst fate.

The Iroquois had entered the weakest side of the palisade and on the other side there was no escape. In all, only three Huron's escaped. The Iroquois left a guard to hold the town. They smeared their faces with the blood of their victims and rushed in the dim light of the early dawn toward the town of St. Louis about a league away.

The three fugitives that had fled St. Louis ran naked through the forest raising the alarm to St. Ignace. The number of inhabitants there was less than seven hundred and of these all who had the strength to escape did so in wild terror for a place of safety. Many of the old and sick were left in their lodges. At this time, there were about eighty warriors who remained. Ignorant of the strength of the Iroquois sang their war songs and were resolved to hold the place to the last.

The two Jesuits stationed at the town, Brebeuf and Lalemant, were urged to escape before the Iroquois arrived. But Brebeuf had no thought of flight. He felt it his duty to cheer on those who fought to defend the mission and open Heaven to those who fell. His colleague, slight of frame and frail in constitution, trembled despite himself; but deep enthusiasm mastered his weakness of nature, and he too, refused to flee.

Scarcely had the sun risen, when like a troop of tigers, the Iroquois rushed to the assault. Yell echoed yell and shot answered shot. The Huron's fought with the utmost desperation, and with arrows, stones, and the few guns they had killed thirty of their assailants, and wounded many more.

Twice the Iroquois recoiled, and twice renewed the attack with unabated ferocity. They swarmed at the foot of the palisades and hacked them with their hatchets until they cut them through in several places. For a time there was a deadly fight at these breaches. Here were two Jesuits, promising Heaven to those who died for the faith, one giving baptism and the other absolution.

At length the Iroquois broke in and captured all the surviving defenders, the Jesuits among the rest. They set the town on fire, and the helpless occupants, who had remained, unable to flee, were consumed in the burning dwellings.

The Iroquois next fell upon the Jesuits, stripping them and binding them fast, they were led back to St. Ignace. Once they arrived, the Iroquois turned their fury on the two Jesuits, beating them savagely with sticks and clubs as they drove them into the town. At the present, there was no time for further torture, they still had more to accomplish.

The victors divided themselves into several bands to burn

the neighboring villages and hunt their fleeing inhabitants. Eventually, they meditated a bolder enterprise, and, in the afternoon, their chiefs sent small parties to reconnoiter Saint Marie for the purpose of attacking it on the next day.

Meanwhile the fugitives of St. Louis were struggling through the soft snow which clogged the forests towards Lake Huron, where the treacherous ice of spring was still not melted. One fear expelled another. They ventured upon it, and pushed forward all that day and all the following night, shivering and famished to find refuge in the towns of the Tobacco Nation.

Ragueneau Bressani and their companions waited in suspense at Saint-Marie. On the one hand, they trembled for Brebeuf and Lalemant; on the other, they looked hourly for an attack. In the evening, when they saw the Iroquois scouts prowling along the edge of the bordering forest, their fears were confirmed. They had with them forty Frenchmen, well-armed, but their palisades and wooden buildings were not fire-proof and they had learned from some of the fugitives the number and ferocity of the invaders. They stood guard all night, praying to the Saints, and above all to their great patron, Saint Joseph, whose festival was close at hand.

In the morning they were somewhat relieved by the arrival of about three hundred Huron warriors. These were converts from La Conception and Saint Madeleine. These Huron's were well armed and full of fight. They were expecting others to join them. Meanwhile, they divided into several bands spreading out into the neighboring forest hoping to waylay parties of Iroquois.

Their expectation was fulfilled. They surprised two hundred of the Iroquois making their way from St. Ignace in advance of the main body to begin an attack on Saint Marie. The Huron's killed many and drove the rest in terror through the snow, chasing them within sight of Saint Marie. The Huron's in the town heard the yells and firing and attacked the Iroquois. They ran for shelter to St. Louis followed closely by the Huron's.

The houses of the town had been burned, but the palisade around them was still standing, though breached and broken. The Iroquois rushed in, but the Huron's were at their heels. Many of the fugitives were captured; the rest killed or put to utter rot. The triumphant Huron's remained masters of the place.

The Iroquois who escaped fled to St. Ignace where they found the main body of the invaders. When the main body of the Iroquois was informed of the disaster that befell their brothers, the whole army turned toward St. Louis to take their revenge.

One of the most famous Native American battles on record occurred. The Huron's within the palisade did not exceed one hundred and fifty. Many had been killed or disabled and many had straggled away. Most of their enemies had guns while the Huron's had few. The Huron's weapons were bows and arrows, war-clubs, hatchets, and knives. The weapons they had were put to good use, sallying repeatedly, fighting like devils, and driving their assailants back again and again.

There are times when the Native American warrior forgets his cautious maxims and throws himself into battle with a mad and reckless ferocity. The desperation of one party, and the fierce courage of both, kept up the fight after the day had come to an end. There was a scout from Saint Marie that, listening from a short distance, observed the battle long into the night.

The principle chief of the Iroquois was severely wounded, and a hundred of their warriors were killed on the spot. Eventually, the Iroquois numbers and persistent fury prevailed. Their only prize was some twenty Huron warriors that were spent with fatigue and faint with loss of blood. The rest of the Huron warriors lay dead around the shattered palisades which they had so valiantly defended. Looking back at the Huron Nation, it was fatuity, not cowardice, which was their ruin.

The lamps burned all night at Saint Marie, and its defenders stood watching till daylight with harquebus in hand. The Jesuits prayed without ceasing and St. Joseph was besieged with invocations. "Those of us who were Jesuits," writes Ragueneau, "each made a vow to say mass in his honor every month for the space of a year; and all the rest bound themselves by vows of penances."

The expected onslaught did not take place. Not an Iroquois appeared. Their victory had been bought too dear, and they had no stomach for more fighting. All the rest of the day, the Eighteenth, stillness, like the dead lull of a tempest followed the turmoil of the day before, as if, said Father Superior, "The country was waiting with fright for some new disaster."

On the following day, the festival of St. Joseph, Huron's came in with tidings that a panic had seized the Iroquois camp and the chiefs could not control it. It was reported that the whole body of the invaders was retreating in disorder, possessed with a vague terror that the Huron's were upon them in force.

They found time, however, for an act of atrocious cruelty. They planted stakes in the bark houses of St. Ignace, and bound to them those of their prisoners whom they meant to sacrifice, male and female, from old age to infancy, husbands, mothers, and children side by side. Then as they retreated, they set fire to the town and laughed with a savage glee at the shrieks of the anguish that rose from the blazing dwellings.

They loaded the rest of their prisoners with their baggage and plunder, and drove them through the forest southward, braining with their hatchets any who gave out on the march. An old woman, who had escaped out of the midst of the flames of St. Ignace, made her way to St. Michel, a large town not far from the desolate site of St. Joseph. Here she found about seven hundred Huron warriors. She set them on the track of the retreating Iroquois and they took up the chase. The Huron's, while they had little beside their bows and arrows, were not eager to overtake the Iroquois armed with their Dutch guns.

They found, as they advanced, the dead bodies of prisoners tomahawked on the march, and others bound fast to trees and half burned by the fagots piled hastily around them. The Iroquois pushed forward with such headlong speed that the pursuers could not, or would not, overtake them, and, after two days, they gave over the attempt.

On the morning of the twentieth, the Jesuits at Saint Marie received full confirmation of the reported retreat of the invaders, and one of them, along with seven armed Frenchmen, set out for the scene of havoc.

They passed St. Louis where the ground was strewn thick with corpses, and, two or three miles farther on, they reached St. Ignace. Here they saw a spectacle of horror. Among the ashes of the burnt town were scattered in profusion the half-consumed bodies of those who had perished in the flames.

Apart from the rest of the destruction, they saw a sight that banished all else from their thoughts; for they found what they had come to find: the scorched and mangled bodies of Brebeuf and Lalemant.

They had previously learned the fate of these Jesuits from Huron prisoners, many of whom had made their escape in the panic and confusion of the Iroquois retreat. They described what they had witnessed and the condition in which the bodies were found confirmed their story.

On the afternoon of the Sixteenth, the day when the two Jesuits were captured, Brebeuf was led apart and bound to a stake. He seemed more concerned for his captive converts than for himself. He addressed these wretched prisoners in a loud voice, exhorting them to suffer patiently, and promising them Heaven as their reward.

The Iroquois were incensed and scorched him for head to toe to silence him. Brebeuf, with the tone of a master, threatened them with the everlasting flames of Hell for persecuting the worshippers of God.

As he continued to speak, with a voice and countenance unchanged, they cut away his lower lip and thrust a red-hot iron down his throat. He held his tall form erect and defiant, showing no sign of pain.

They tried another means to overcome him. They led out Lalemant that Brebeuf might see him tortured. They had tied strips of bark smeared with pitch about his neck and naked body. When he saw the condition of his Superior, he could not hide his agitation and called out to him with a broken voice in the words of St. Paul, "We are made a spectacle to the world, to angels and to men." He threw himself at Brebeuf's feet; the Iroquois seized him, made him fast to a stake, and set fire to the bark that enveloped him. As the flames rose, he threw his arms upward and made a supplication to Heaven.

The Iroquois next hung around Brebeuf's neck a collar made of hatchets heated red-hot, but the indomitable priest stood like a rock. A Huron in the crowd, who had been a convert of the mission but was now an Iroquois by adoption, called out with malice of a renegade to pour boiling water over their heads. The Huron said, "They poured cold water on us for so many years."

The kettle was slung, the water boiled, and, when it was ready the boiling water was poured slowly over the heads of the two missionaries. "We baptize you," they cried, "that you may be happy in Heaven, for nobody can be saved without a good baptism." Brebeuf would not flinch; so in a rage, they cut strips of flesh from his limbs and devoured them before his eyes.

Other Huron's called out to him, "You told us that the more one suffers on earth, the happier he is in Heaven. We wish to make you happy; we torment you because we love you, and you should thank us for it."

After a succession of other revolting tortures, they scalped him. Finally, he died. When they noticed that he was dead, they laid open his breast. A crowd came about to drink his blood. It was believed among the Iroquois that drinking the blood of a valiant enemy would pass on to them his courage. A chief then tore out his heart and devoured it.

Jean de Brebeuf was the founder of the Huron mission and its truest hero and its greatest martyr. To the last he refused to flinch, and his death was the astonishment of his tormentors.

Lalemant, physically weak from childhood, and slender almost to emaciation, was constitutionally unequal to a display of fortitude like that of his colleague. When Brebeuf finally died, he was led back to the house whence he had been taken and tortured there all night. In the morning, one of the Iroquois, growing tired of the protracted entertainment, killed him with a hatchet.

It was reported that at times he seemed beside himself, and then he would rally with his hands uplifted and offer his sufferings to Heaven as a sacrifice. Brebeuf had lived less than four hours under the torture, while Lalemant survived it for nearly seventeen.

The bodies of the two missionaries were carried to Saint Marie and buried in the cemetery there, but the skull of Brebeuf was preserved as a relic. His family sent from France a silver bust of their martyred kinsman, in the base of which was a recess to contain the skull. To this day, the bust and relic within are preserved with pious care by the nuns of the Hotel Dieu at Quebec.

These are just some of the examples that describe the atmosphere and the dangers the populations of New France were facing about the time of Adam Dollard's arrival.

Late in the preceding autumn the Iroquois had taken the warpath in force. At the end of November, two escaped prisoners came to St. Joseph with the news that a band of three hundred warriors was hovering in the Huron forests. They were debating as to whether to invade the island or to attack the towns of the Tobacco Nation in the valleys of the Blue Mountains. The Father Superior, Ragueneau, sent a runner thither in all haste to warn the inhabitants of their danger.

There were, at this time, two missions in the Tobacco Nation, St. Jean and St. Matthias, the latter under the change of the Jesuits Garreau and Grelon, and the former under that of Garnier and Chabanel.

St. Jean, the principal seat of the mission of the same name, was a town of five or six hundred families. Its population was moreover greatly augmented by the bands of fugitive Huron's who had taken refuge there.

When the warriors were warned by Ragueneau's messenger of a probable attack from the Iroquois, they were far from being daunted. The Huron warriors were confident in their numbers and awaited the enemy in one of their fits of valor.

At St. Jean all was paint, feathers, and uproar. There was singing, dancing, howling, and stamping. Quivers were filled, knives whetted, and tomahawks sharpened. But when after two days of eager expectancy the enemy did not appear, the warriors lost patience. Thinking, and probably with reason, the Iroquois were afraid of them, they resolved to take the offensive. With yelps and whoops they rushed into the forest, where the branches were gray and bare, and the ground was thickly covered with snow.

They pushed rapidly until the following day, but could not discover their enemy, who had made a wide circuit, and was approaching the town from another direction. Not too far from the town, the Iroquois captured a Tobacco Indian and his squaw in the surrounding forest. After being intimidated by the threat of torture, they told their captives about the defenseless condition of the town and its only occupants were women, children, and old men. The delighted Iroquois no longer hesitated, but silently and swiftly pushed on toward the town.

It was two o'clock in the afternoon on the Seventh of December. Chabanel had left the place a day or two before in obedience to a message from Ragueneau, and Garnier was at the mission alone. He was making the rounds among the houses visiting the sick and instructing his converts. Suddenly, the din of a war whoop rose from the borders of the clearing, and, in an instant, the town was mad with terror. Children and girls rushed back and forth blind with fright; women grabbed their infants and fled into the forest.

Garnier ran to his chapel where a few of his converts had sought asylum. He gave them his benediction, instructed them to hold fast to the faith and told them to run for their lives while there was still time. Afterward, he ran back to the houses, moving from one to another, giving absolution or baptism to all he found. As he was coming out of one of the houses an Iroquois shot him with three balls through the body and the thigh. The warrior tore off his cassock and rushed on in pursuit of other fugitives.

Garnier lay on the ground for a moment as if stunned, and then recovering his senses, it was witnessed that he was seen kneeling. Not too far from his position was a Huron, mortally wounded, but still showing signs of life. The priest dragged himself towards the dying Indian to give him absolution, but his strength failed and he fell to the ground. He rose once again and crept forward when he was spotted by a party of Iroquois who rushed upon him. They split his head with two blows of a hatchet, stripped him, and left his body on the ground.

At this time the whole town was on fire. The warriors, fearing that the absent Huron warriors might return, scattered firebrands everywhere and threw children alive into the burning houses. They killed many more and, taking some prisoners, made a hasty retreat into the forest, killing those who could not keep up the march. St. Jean lay waste thickly strewn with blackened corpses of the slain.

Later that evening, parties of fugitives reached St. Matthias with tidings of the catastrophe. The town was wild with alarm in expectation of an attack. In the morning, scouts came in and reported the Iroquois had retreated. Garreau and Grelon set out with a party of converts to visit the scene of destruction. For a long time they looked for the body of Garnier and eventually they found him where he had fallen. He was so scorched and disfigured that they hardly recognized him. The two Jesuits wrapped his body in a part of their own clothing. The Huron converts dug a grave on the spot where his church had once stood, and here they buried him.

Thus, at the age of forty-four, died Charles Garnier, the favorite child of wealthy noble parents, nursed in Parisian luxury and ease, then living and dying a more willing exile, amid the hardships and horrors of the Huron wilderness. His life and death are his best eulogy. Brebeuf was the lion of the Huron mission, and Garnier was the lamb, but the lamb was as fearless as the lion.

When, on the following morning, the warriors of St. Jean returned from their pursuit of the Iroquois war party and saw their desolated homes and the ghastly relics of their murdered families, they seated themselves amid the ruin, silent and motionless as statues of bronze, with heads bowed down and eyes fixed on the ground. There they remained through the day. Tears and wailing were for the women—this was mourning of warriors.

Garnier's colleague, Chabanel, had been recalled from St. Jean by an order from Father Superior, who thought it needless to expose the life of more than one priest in a position of so much danger. He stopped on his way at St. Matthias, and on the morning of the Seventh of December, the day of the attack, left that town with several Christian Huron's. The journey was rough and difficult. They proceeded through the forest about eighteen miles, and then encamped in the snow. The Huron's fell asleep, but Chabanel, from an apprehension of danger, remained awake. About midnight he heard a strange sound in the distance, a confusion of fierce voices mingled with songs and outcries. It was the Iroquois on their retreat with their prisoners, some of whom were defiantly singing their war-songs.

Chabanel awakened his companions who instantly took flight. He attempted to follow, but could not keep pace with the light-footed Huron's, who returned to St. Matthias and reported as to what had occurred. They said that Chabanel had taken another direction in order to reach St. Joseph. His brother Jesuits were for some time ignorant of what had befallen him. At length a Huron who had been converted admitted that he had met him in the forest and aided him with his canoe to cross a river, which had lain in his path. Some supposed that he had lost his way and perished from cold and hunger; but others were of a different opinion. Their suspicion was confirmed some time afterwards by the Huron who confessed that he had killed Chabanel and thrown his body into the river before robbing him of his clothes. The Huron declared that his motive was hatred of the Faith, which, in his opinion, had caused the ruin of the Huron's.

The priest, before leaving Saint Marie on the Wye to go to his post in the Tobacco Nation, had written to his brother that he was sure he was destined to the fires of the Iroquois. He had added that though he as naturally timid, he was now wholly indifferent to danger, and he expressed the belief that only a superhuman power could have wrought such a change in him.

Garreau and Grelon, at their mission of St. Matthias, were exposed to other dangers than those of the Iroquois. Word was being spread about that not only were they magicians, but they had a secret understanding with the enemy. A nocturnal council was called and their deaths were decreed. In the morning, a furious crowd gathered before a lodge which they were about to enter. The Huron put forth a screeching and yelling much like when they compelled a prisoner to run the gantlet.

The two Jesuits, showing no sign of fear, passed through the crowd and entered the lodge unharmed. Hatchets were brandished over them, but no one would be the first to strike. Their converts were amazed at their escape and ascribed it to a spiritual protection.

The Huron missionaries were doubly in danger from the Huron, who should have been their friends, as they were from the Iroquois.

Six

*A*bout this time too, the Iroquois had set their sights on exterminating their Huron enemies. For all practical reasons, all was over with the Huron's. The Iroquois were dominating all of New France and the territory to the north around the Great Lakes.

The Huron's were without a leader, without organization, without union, crazed with fright and paralyzed with misery. They yielded to their doom without resistance. Their only thought at this time was flight.

Within two weeks after the disasters of St. Ignace and St. Louis, fifteen Huron towns were abandoned. The greater number were burned to prevent them giving shelter to the Iroquois. The last year's harvest had been poor. The Huron's had little or no food, and they left behind them the fields which were their only hope of obtaining it.

In bands, large and small, some roamed northward and eastward, through the half-thawed wilderness; some hid themselves on the rocks or islands of Lake Huron; some sought asylum among the Tobacco Nation; a few joined the Neutrals on the north of Lake Erie. The Huron, as a nation, ceased to exist.

Saint Marie had been covered by large fortified towns which lay between it and the Iroquois, but these were all destroyed, some by the enemy and some by their own people, and the Jesuits were left alone to bear the brunt of the next attack. There was no reason for their remaining at Saint Marie.

Saint Marie had been built as a basis for the missions, but its occupation was now gone. The flock had fled from the shepherds and its existence no longer had an objective. If the priest stayed to be butchered, they would perish, not as martyrs, but as fools. The Jesuits now knew what they had to do and it was as clear as it was bitter. Saint Marie must be abandoned.

The Jesuits believed that since the birth of Christianity, the Faith has not been planted except in the midst of suffering and crosses. They further believed that the desolation consoled them, and in the midst of persecution which assailed them that God had never had more tender love for them than at that moment.

Several of the Jesuits set out to follow and console the scattered bands of fugitive Huron's. One embarked in a canoe and coasted the dreary shores of Lake Huron northward, among the wild labyrinth of rocks and islets where his previous flock had sought refuge. Another priest accompanied a band of half-famished proselytes through the forest and shared their miserable roving's through the thickets and among the mountains. Those who remained took counsel together at Saint Marie. After much discussion, it was decided to establish a new seat of the mission on the Grand Manitoulin Island, called by them "Isle Saint Marie" and by the Huron's "Ekaentoton."

The island lay near the northern shores of Lake Huron and by its location would give a ready access to a number of Algonquin tribes along the borders of these inland seas. Moreover, it would bring the Jesuits and their flock nearer to the French settlements by the route of the Ottawa River. In addition, the fishing was good and some of the Jesuits who were acquainted with that island also made a favorable report on its soil for agriculture.

About the time the remnants of Saint Marie were about to resettle the mission, twelve Huron chiefs arrived and requested an interview with the Father Superior and his fellow Jesuits. The conference lasted three hours. The chiefs declared that many of the scattered Huron's had determined to reunite and form a settlement on a neighboring island in the lake, called by the Jesuits "Isle of St. Joseph." However, the chiefs pointed out that in order to reunite that they needed the aid of the Fathers.

The chiefs made the case that without the Jesuits, they were helpless. But with them, however, they could hold their ground and repel the attacks of the Iroquois. They urged their plea in language which Ragueneau described as pathetic and eloquent, and to confirm their words, they gave him ten large collars of wampum, saying, "These are the voices of our wives and children." They made their point. The Jesuits abandoned their former plan and promised to join the Huron's on the Isle of St. Joseph.

They had built a small vessel and embarked with as many stores as it would hold. The greater part was placed on a large raft made for the purpose, like one of the rafts of timber which every summer would float down the St. Lawrence and the Ottawa.

Here was their stock of corn, in part the produce of their own fields, and in part bought from the Huron's in former years of plenty. There were also pictures, vestments, sacred vessels and images, weapons, ammunition, tools, goods for barter with the other tribes, cattle, swine, and poultry.

Saint Marie was stripped of everything that could be moved. To ensure that it couldn't harbor the Iroquois, they set it on fire and saw consumed in an hour the results of ten years of toil.

It was near sunset on the Fourteenth of June. The houseless band descended to the mouth of the Wye, went on board their raft, pushed it from the shore, and, with sweeps and oars, urged it on its way all night.

The lake was calm and the weather fair, but it crept so slowly over the water that it took several days for it to reach their destination, twenty miles distant.

Near the entrance of Matchedash Bay lay the three islands now known as Faith, Hope, and Charity. Of these, Charity or Christian Island, called Ahoendoe by the Huron's and St. Joseph by the Jesuits, is by far the largest. It was eight miles wide when the Huron's sought refuge there and was a densely covered primeval forest.

The Jesuits landed with their men, some forty soldiers, laborers, and three hundred Huron families. They erected wigwams, sheds of bark, and slung their kettles over a fire. They had little energy. After their initial settlement, they lay around in groups of famished wretches with dark, haggard visages and uncombed hair. They had not been completely idle for they made some rough clearings and planted a little corn.

The arrival of the Jesuits gave them new hope, and weakened as they were with famine, they set themselves to the task of hewing and planting palisades. The Jesuits chose a favorable spot and began to clear the ground to mark out lines for a fort.

The Jesuit men who were working without pay labored with admirable spirit, and before winter had built a square, a bastioned fort of solid masonry, with a deep ditch and walls about twelve feet high. Within it were a small chapel, houses for lodging, and a well. Detached redoubts were also built near at hand, where French harquebusiers could aid in defending the adjacent Huron village.

Though the island was called St. Joseph, the fort, like that of the Wye, received the name of Saint Marie. The island, thanks to the vigilance of the French, escaped attack throughout the summer, but Iroquois scalping-parties ranged the neighboring shores, killing stragglers and keeping the Huron's in perpetual alarm.

As the winter drew near, great numbers, who, trembling and by stealth, had gathered a miserable subsistence among the northern forests and islands, rejoined their countrymen at St. Joseph, until eight thousand expatriated Huron's were gathered there under the protection of the French fort. They were housed in a hundred or more bark dwellings, each containing ten families. Here were widows without children, and children without parents, for famine and the Iroquois had proved more deadly enemies than the pestilence which a few years before had wasted their towns.

Of this multitude, few had strength enough to labor, scarcely any had made provision for the winter, and numbers were already perishing from want, dragging themselves from house to house, like living skeletons. The Jesuits had spared no effort doing everything they could to assist these desperate people. They sent men during the autumn to buy smoked fish from the Northern Algonquin's, and employed them to gather acorns in the woods. They succeeded in collecting six hundred bushels. To diminish the bitterness, the Huron's boiled it with ashes, or the Jesuits served it out to them pounded and mixed with corn.

As winter advanced, the Huron houses became a frightful spectacle. The inmates were dying by the scores daily. The Jesuits and their men buried the bodies, and some of the Huron's dug them up from the earth or the snow and fed on them, sometimes in secret and sometimes openly. Notwithstanding their superstitious feasts on the bodies of their enemies, their repugnance and horror were extreme at the thought of devouring those relatives and friends. Eventually, an epidemic appeared as a result of the famine. Before spring, about half their numbers were dead.

Meanwhile, though the cold was intense and the snow several feet high, not an hour was free from the danger of the Iroquois. The French sentries walked the ramparts from sunset to daybreak.

The Jesuits rose before dawn and spent the time until sunrise in their private devotions. Then the bell of their chapel rang, and the Huron's came in crowds at the call, their misery had softened their hearts and nearly all on the island were now Christian.

There was a mass followed by a prayer and a few words of exhortation, then the hearers dispersed to make room for others. Thus the little chapel was filled ten to twelve times until all had had their turn.

Meanwhile other Jesuits were hearing confessions and giving advice and encouragement in private according to the needs of the applicant. This lasted until nine o'clock when all the participants returned to the village. The Jesuits would then visit the houses and pass out a few acorns, a small quantity of boiled maize, or a fragment of smoked fish. Two hours before sunset the bell of the chapel would ring again and the religious exercises of the morning were repeated.

As the miserable winter wore away the spring brought new fears and new necessities. As spring approached, the starving multitude on the Isle of St. Joseph grew reckless with hunger. Along the main shore, in spots where the sun lay warm, the spring fisheries had already begun and the melting snow was uncovering the acorns in the woods.

There was danger everywhere, for bands of Iroquois were again on the track of their prey. The miserable Huron's, gnawed with inexorable famine, and stood in the dilemma of a deadly peril and an assured death. They chose the former, and, early in March, they began to leave their island and cross to the mainland to gather what sustenance they could. The ice was still thick, but the advancing season had softened it. As a body of Huron's was crossing, it broke under their feet. Some were drowned, while others dragged themselves out, drenched and pierced with cold, to die miserably on the frozen lake.

Other parties were more fortunate and gained the shore safely. Eventually, they began fishing, divided into companies of eight to ten. In the surrounding forest, the Iroquois were in wait for them.

A large band of warriors had already made their way through the ice and snow from their towns in Central New York. They surprised the Huron fishermen, surrounded them, and cut them to pieces without resistance. The Iroquois hunted down the few that managed to get away with such persistency and skill that of all who had gone over to the main the Jesuits knew of only one who managed to escape.

"My pen," wrote Ragueneau "has no ink black enough to describe the fury of the Iroquois." Still the goading of famine was relentless and irresistible. "It is said," added the Father Superior, "that hunger will drive wolves from the forest. So, too, our starving Huron's were driven out of a town which had become an abode of horror. It was the end of Lent. If these poor Christians could have had but acorns and water to keep their fast upon! On Easter Day we caused them to make a general confession. On the following morning they went away, leaving all their little possessions; and most of them declared publicly that they made us their heirs, knowing well that they were near their end. And, in fact, only a few days passed before we heard of the disaster which we had foreseen. These poor people fell into ambuscades of our Iroquois enemies. Some were killed on the spot; some were dragged into captivity; women and children were burned. A few made their escape, and spread dismay and panic everywhere. A week after, another band was overtaken by the same fate. Go where they would, they met with slaughter on all sides. Famine pursued them, or they encountered an enemy crueler than cruelty itself; and, to crown their misery, they heard that two great armies of Iroquois were on the way to exterminate them. Despair was universal."

The Jesuits at St. Joseph knew not what course to take. The doom of their flock seemed inevitable. When dismay and dependency were at their height, two of the principal Huron chiefs came to the fort and asked for an interview with Ragueneau and his companions. They told them that the Huron's had held a council the night before and decided to abandon the island. Some would disperse in the most remote and inaccessible forests; others would take refuge on the Grand Manitoulin Island; others would try to reach the Andastes; and still others would seek safety in adoption and incorporation with the Iroquois themselves.

"Take courage, brother," continued one of the chiefs, addressing Ragueneau. "You can save us, if you will but resolve on a bold step. Choose a place where you can gather us together, and prevent this dispersion of our people. Turn your eyes towards Quebec, and transport thither what is left of this ruined country. Do not wait till war and famine have destroyed us to the last man. We are in your hands. Death has taken from you more than ten thousand of us. If you wait longer, not one will remain alive; and then you will be sorry that you did not save those whom you might have snatched from danger, and who showed you the means of doing so. If you do as we wish, we will form a church under the protection of the fort at Quebec. Our faith will not be extinguished. The examples of the French and Algonquians will encourage us in our duty, and their charity will relieve some of our misery. At least, we shall sometimes find a morsel of bread for our children, who so long have had nothing but bitter roots and acorns to keep them alive."

The Jesuits were deeply moved. They consulted together again and again, and prayed in turn during forty hours, without ceasing, that their minds might be enlightened. At length they resolved to grant the petition of the two chiefs, and save the poor remnant of the Huron's by leading them to an asylum where there was at least a hope of safety. Their resolution once taken, they pushed their preparations with all speed, lest the Iroquois might learn their purpose, and lie in wait to cut them off.

Canoes were made ready, and on the Tenth of June they began the voyage with all their French followers and about three hundred Huron's. The Huron mission was abandon.

"It was not without tears," wrote Father Superior, "that we left the country of our hopes and our hearts, where our brethren had gloriously shed their blood."

The fleet of canoes held its melancholy way along the shores where two years before had been the seat of one of the chief Huron communities of the continent, and where now all was a waste of death and desolation.

They steered northward, along the eastern coast of the Georgian Bay with its countless rocky inlets; everywhere they saw the traces of the Iroquois. When they reached Lake Nipissing, they found it deserted. Nothing remained of the Algonquians who dwelt on its shore, except the ashes of their burnt wigwams. A little further on there was a fort built of trees where the Iroquois who made this desolation had spent the winter. A league or two beyond there was another fort.

The River Ottawa was solitude. The Algonquians of Allumette

Island and on the shores adjacent had all been killed or driven away, never again to return.

"When I came up this great river only thirteen years ago," wrote Ragueneau, "I found it bordered with Algonquian tribes who knew no God, and, in their infidelity, thought themselves gods on earth; for they had all that they desired, abundance of fish and game, and a prosperous trade with allied nations: besides, they were the terror of their enemies. But since they have embraced the Faith and adored the cross of Christ, He has given them a heavy share in this cross, and made them a prey to misery, torture, and a cruel death. They are a people swept from the face of the earth. Our only consolation is that as they died Christians, they have a part in the inheritance of the true children of God, who scourged every one He receives."

As the voyagers descended the river, they had a serious alarm. Their scouts came in and reported that they had found fresh footprints of men in the forest. These proved, however, to be tracks, not of enemies, but of friends.

In the preceding autumn Bressani had gone down to the French settlements with about twenty Huron's and was now returning with them, and twice their number of armed Frenchmen, for the defense of the mission. His scouts had also been alarmed by discovering the footprints of Ragueneau's Huron's, and for some time the two parties stood on their guard, each taking the other for the enemy.

When at length they discovered their mistake, they met with embraces and rejoicing. Bressani and his Frenchmen had come too late. All was over with the Huron's and the Huron mission, and it was useless to go farther; they joined Ragueneau's party and retraced their course for the settlements.

A day or two before, they had had a sharp taste of the enemy.

Ten Iroquois warriors had spent the winter in a little fort of felled trees on the borders of the Ottawa, hunting for subsistence and waiting to waylay some passing canoe of Huron's, Algonquians, or Frenchmen. Bressani's party outnumbered them six to one, but the Iroquois were resolved to attack them.

Late at night, the French and Huron's lay encamped in the forest, sleeping around their fires. They had set guards. However, it seemed they were drowsy or negligent. The ten Iroquois, watching for a convenient time, approached with the stealth of lynxes and glided like shadows into the midst of the camp. By the dull glow of the smoldering fires, they could distinguish the figures of their victims.

Suddenly, they screeched the war-whoop, and struck like lightening with their hatchets on the sleepers. Seven were killed before the rest could spring to their weapons. Bressani leaped up and received three wounds to his head. Eventually, the Iroquois were surrounded and a desperate fight ensued in the dark. Six of them were killed on the spot and two were made prisoners. The remaining two broke free and escaped into the forest.

The group finally reached Ville-Marie, but the Huron's refused to remain in a spot so exposed to the Iroquois. After resting for a day, they all descended the St. Lawrence River. On the Twenty-Eighth of July they reached Quebec. They were welcomed by the Ursuline's and the inhabitants of the town shared their resources with these exiled Huron's. Food was scarce at Quebec and the Jesuits had to bear the chief burden of keeping the sufferers alive.

But if famine was an evil, the Iroquois were a far greater one, for, while the western nations of their confederacy were engrossed with the destruction of the Huron's, the Mohawks kept up incessant attacks on the Algonquians and the French.

A party of Christian Algonquians, chiefly from Sillery, planned a stroke of retaliation and set out for Mohawk country, marching cautiously and sending forward scouts to scour the forest.

One of these, a Huron, suddenly fell in with a large Iroquois war party. Seeing that he could not escape, he formed an instant villainous plan to save him. He ran towards the enemy, crying out that he had long been looking for them and was delighted that he found them. He told them that his nation, the Huron's, had come to an end. "Therefore, my country was now the country of the Iroquois, where so many of my kinsmen and friends had been adopted. I come with no other thought than to joining and turning Iroquois as they had done."

The Iroquois demanded to know if he had come alone. He answered, "No," and said that in order to accomplish his purpose; he had joined an Algonquian war party that was in the forest not too far off. The Iroquois were delighted and demanded to be shown where they were.

"The Judas," as the Jesuits called him, at once complied. The Algonquians were surprised by a sudden onset and routed with severe losses. The treacherous Huron was well treated by the Iroquois and was adopted into their nation.

Not too long after this instant, he came to Quebec with the thought of some further treachery to rejoin the French. A sharp cross-questioning put him into confusion and he presently confessed his guilt. He was sentenced to death, and the sentence was executed by one of own countrymen, who split his head with a hatchet.

In the course of the summer, the French at Trois Rivieres became aware that a band of Iroquois were prowling in the neighborhood, and sixty men went out to meet them. Far from retreating, the Iroquois, who were about twenty-five in number, got out of their canoes and took positions, waist-deep in the mud and water, among the tall rushes at the edge of the river. Here they fought stubbornly, and kept the Frenchmen at bay. Eventually, finding themselves hard pressed, they entered their canoes again and paddled off. The French rowed after them but soon became separated in the chase; however, the Iroquois returned and made a desperate fight only to retreat again. They repeated this tactic several times before killing several of the best French soldiers and making their escape.

Their leader in this affair was a famous half-breed, known as the "Flemish Bastard," who is styled by Ragueneau as "an abomination of sin and a monster produced between a heretic Dutch father and a pagan mother."

In the forests far north of Trois Rivieres dwelt the tribe called the Atticamegues, or Nation of the White Fish. From their remote position, and the difficult nature of the intervening country, they thought themselves safe, but a band of Iroquois, marching on snowshoes a distance of twenty days' journey northward from the St. Lawrence, fell upon one of their camps in the winter and made a general butchery of the inmates.

The tribe, however, still held its ground for a time, and, being all good Catholics, gave their missionary, Father Buteux, an urgent invitation to visit them in their own country. Buteux, who had long been stationed at Trois Rivieres, was in ill health, and for years had rarely been free from some form of bodily malady. Nevertheless, he acceded to their request, and, before the opening of spring, made a remarkable journey on snowshoes into the depth of this frozen wilderness.

In the following year, he repeated the undertaking. With him were a party of Atticamegues and several Frenchmen. Game was exceedingly scarce and they were forced by hunger to separate. A Huron convert and a Frenchman named Fontarabie remained with the missionary. The snows had melted, and all the streams were swollen. The three travelers, in a small birch canoe, pushed their way up a turbulent river where falls and rapids were numerous. Many times throughout the day they were forced to carry their bark vessel and their baggage through the forests and thickets and over rocks and precipices.

On the Tenth of May, they made two such portages, and soon after reaching a third falls, again lifted their canoe from the water. They toiled through the naked forest, among the black trees, over tangled roots, green spongy mosses, moldering leaves and rotten tree trunks while the cataract foamed below.

The Huron led the way with the canoe on his head, while Buteux and the other Frenchman followed with the baggage. Suddenly, they were set upon by a troop of Iroquois, who had crouched behind thickets, rocks, and fallen trees, to waylay them. The Huron was captured before he had time to flee. Buteux and the Frenchman tried to escape, but were instantly shot down, the Jesuit receiving two balls in the breast. The Iroquois rushed upon them, mangled their bodies with tomahawks and swords, stripped them, and threw their bodies into the torrent.

Seven

*I*roquois bullets and tomahawks had killed the Huron's by the hundreds, but famine and disease had killed more. The miseries of the starving crowd on the Isle of St. Joseph had been shared in an equal degree by smaller bands, which had wintered in remote and secret retreats of the wilderness.

Of those who survived the season of death, many were so weakened that they could not endure the hardships of a wandering life, which was new to them. The Huron's lived by agriculture. Their fields and crops were destroyed, and they were so hunted from place to place that they could rarely till the soil. Game was very scarce, and without agriculture, the country could support only a scanty and scattered population of that which maintained a struggling existence in the wilderness of the lower St. Lawrence. The mortality among the exiles was enormous.

The Huron's failed to exist within their ancient domain. Some had sought refuge among the Neutrals and the Eries, while others succeeded in reaching the Andastes along the Susquehanna River.

The inhabitants of St. Michel and St. Jean Baptist contrived to open communications with the Seneca Nation of the Iroquois. They promised to change their nationality and become Seneca for the price of their lives. The victors accepted their proposal, and the inhabitant of these two towns, joined by a few other Huron's, migrated in a body to the Seneca country. They were not distributed among different villages, but were allowed to form a town by themselves, where they were afterwards joined by some prisoners of the Neutral Nation. They identified themselves with the Iroquois in all facets of life except religion. They held fast to their Catholic faith. Eighteen years later, a Jesuit missionary found that many of them were still Catholics in good standing.

The division of the Huron's, called the Tobacco Nation, due to their isolated position among the mountains, and had held their ground longer than the rest. But eventually, they too were compelled to flee, together with other Huron's who had taken refuge with them.

They made their way northward, and settled on the Island of Michilimackinac, where they were joined by the Ottawa's, who, with other Algonquians, had been driven by fear of the Iroquois from the western shores of Lake Huron and the banks of the River Ottawa. At Michilimackinac the Huron's and their allies were again attacked by the Iroquois, and, after remaining for several years, they made another move. They took possession of the islands at the mouth of the Green Bay of Lake Michigan. Even here their old enemy did not leave them in peace. Out of necessity, they fortified themselves on the mainland. A short time later, they migrated south and west.

This brought them into contact with the Illinois, an Algonquian people, at the time very numerous, but, like many other tribes, were doomed to a rapid decrease in population from wars with other Native American nations.

Continuing their migration westward, the Huron's and Ottawa's reached the Mississippi, where they fell in with the Sioux. After a while, they quarreled with those fierce children of the prairie who drove them from their country.

They retreated to the southwestern extremity of Lake Superior and settled on Point Saint Esprit or Shagwamigon Point near the islands of the Twelve Apostles. The Sioux continued to harass them, so they left that place. They returned once again to Michilimackinac, where they settled, not on the island, but on the neighboring Point St. Ignace, at the northern extremity of the great peninsula of Michigan.

The greater part of them eventually moved to what is now Detroit and Sandusky, where they lived under the name of Wyandots.

When Ragueneau and his party left the Isle St. Joseph for Quebec, the greater number of the Huron's chose to remain. They took possession of the stone fort which the French had abandoned, and where, with reasonable vigilance, they could maintain themselves against attack.

In the succeeding autumn a small band of Iroquois war party crossed over to the island and built a fort of felled trees in the woods. The Huron's attacked them, and the Iroquois made a fierce defense, but eventually, they retreated with little loss.

Soon afterward, a much larger band of Onondaga Iroquois approached undiscovered, built a fort on the mainland opposite the island, and concealed it from sight in the forest. Here they waited to waylay any party of Huron's who might venture ashore.

A Huron war chief named Annaotaha, whose life is described as a succession of conflicts and adventures, and who is said to have been always in luck, landed with a few companions. They fell into an ambush of the Iroquois. He prepared to defend himself when they called out to him that they came not as enemies, but as friends. They assured him that they brought wampum-belts and presents to persuade the Huron's to forget the past, go back with them to their country, become their adopted countrymen, and live with them as one nation.

Annaotaha suspected treachery, but concealed his distrust. He advanced towards the Iroquois with an air of the utmost confidence. They received him with open arms and pressed him to accept their invitation. He replied that there were older and wiser men among the Huron's, whose councils all the people followed, and that they ought to lay the proposal before them. He proceeded to advise them to keep him as a hostage and send over his companions with some of their chiefs to open negotiation.

His apparent frankness completely deceived them, and they insisted that he himself should go to the Huron village, while his companions remained as hostages. He set out accordingly with three companions of the principal Iroquois.

When he reached the village, he gave the whoop of one who brings good tidings, and proclaimed with a loud voice that the hearts of their enemies had changed, that the Iroquois would become their countrymen and brothers, and that they should exchange their miseries for a life of peace and plenty in a fertile and prosperous land.

The whole Huron population, full of joyful excitement, crowded about him and the three envoys were conducted into the principal lodge and feasted on the best that the village could provide.

Annaotaha took the opportunity to take aside four or five of the principal chiefs, and secretly told them of his suspicions that the Iroquois were plotting their destruction under the cover of peace overtures. He recommended that they meet treachery with treachery. He then explained his plan, which was approved by the other chiefs. They begged Annaotaha to execute the plan.

Annaotaha now had criers to proclaim through the village that everyone should get ready to immigrate in a few days to the country of their new friends. The squaws began their preparations at once, and all was bustle and alacrity, for the Huron's was no less deceived than were the Iroquois envoys.

During one or two succeeding days, many messages and visits passed between the Huron's and the Iroquois, whose confidence was such, that thirty-seven of their best warriors came over in a body to the Huron village. Annaotaha's time had come. He and the chiefs who were in on the secret plan gave the word to the Huron warriors, who, at a signal, were to raise the war whoop, rush upon the Iroquois warriors, and cut them to pieces. One of them, who lingered for a time, admitted before he died that Annaotaha's suspicions were exactly correct. The Iroquois had designed a plan to massacre or capture all of the Huron's. Three of the Iroquois, immediately before the slaughter began, were warned by Annaotaha of their danger in time to make their escape. The year before, he had been captured with Brebeuf and Lalemant at the town of St. Louis, and had owed his life to these three warriors to whom he now paid back the debt of gratitude. The three informed the Iroquois on the mainland of what had befallen their countrymen and were aghast at the catastrophe and fled home in a panic.

Here was a sweet morsel of vengeance. The miseries of the Huron's were lighted up with a brief gleam of joy, but it behooved them to make a timely retreat from their island before the Iroquois came to extract a bloody retribution.

Towards spring, while the lake was still frozen, many of them escaped on the ice, while another party afterwards followed in canoes. Those didn't have the strength to walk nor had canoes to transport them, remained behind and were soon massacred by the Iroquois.

The fugitives directed their course to Grand Manitoulin Island where they remained for a short period of time. Then, a number of about four hundred descended the Ottawa and rejoined their countrymen who had gone to Quebec the year before.

These united parties, joined from time to time by a few other fugitives, formed a settlement on land belonging to the Jesuits near the southwestern extremity of the Isle of Orleans, immediately below Quebec. Here the Jesuits built a fort like the one on Isle of St. Joseph with a chapel and a small house for the missionaries. The bark dwellings of the Huron's were clustered around the protecting ramparts. Tools and seeds were given to them, and they were encouraged to cultivate the soil.

Gradually, they rallied from their dejection, and the mission settlement was beginning to wear an appearance of thrift, when in 1656, the Iroquois made a descent upon them and carried off a large number of captives under the very cannon of Quebec. The French were reluctant to fire on them, thus they may take revenge upon the Jesuits who were at a time in their country.

This calamity was four years before when the best Huron warriors including their leader, Annaotaha, were slain fighting side by side with Adam Dollard at the battle of Long Sault.

The attenuated colony, replenished by some straggling bands of the same nation, and still numbering several hundred persons, migrated to Quebec after the inroad in 1656, and lodged in a square enclosure of palisades close to the fort. Here they remained for about ten years, when, the danger of the times having diminished, they were once again removed to a place called Notre-Dame de Foy.

Six years after, when the soil was impoverished and the wood in the neighborhood exhausted, they again changed their abode, under the auspices of the Jesuits, and settled at Old Lorette nine miles from Quebec.

Chaumonot was at this time their missionary. He had professed a special devotion to Our Lady of Lorette, who, in his boyhood, had cured him, as he believed, of a distressing malady. He had always cherished the idea of building a chapel in honor of her in Canada, after the model of the Holy House of Lorette.

Chaumonot presented his plan to his brother Jesuits, who were delighted with it. The chapel was begun at once. It was constructed of brick and it stood in the center of a quadrangle, the four sides of which were formed by the bark dwellings of the Huron's, ranged with perfect order in straight lines.

But the Huron's were not destined to remain permanently even here, for they removed to a place four miles distant. It was an undeveloped spot covered by a primitive forest, and surrounded by a deep and tortuous ravine. It was here where the St. Charles foamed white as a snow-drift, over the black ledges, and where the sunlight struggled through matted boughs of the pine and fir, to bask for brief moments on the mossy rocks or flash on the hurrying waters.

Of the four kindred communities, two at least, the Huron's and the Neutrals, were probably superior in numbers to the Iroquois. Either one of these with proper leadership could have held its ground against them, or the two united could easily have crippled them from presenting a threat.

But these so-called nations were mere aggregations of villages and families, with nothing that deserved to be called a government. They were subjected to panics, because the part attacked by an enemy could never rely with confidence on prompt help from the rest, and when once broken, they could not be rallied, because there was no central government.

The Iroquois, on the other hand, had organization with which the ideas and habits of several generations were interwoven, and they had leaders with a keen sense of perception for war and peace. They discussed all questions of policy with the coolest deliberation, and knew how to turn a profit even when imperfections in their plan of government seemed to promise only weakness and discord.

Thus, any nation, or any large town, of their confederacy, could make a separate war or a separate peace with a foreign nation, or any part of it. Some member of the league, as, for example, the Cayugas, would make a covenant of friendship with the enemy. And, while the infatuated victims were thus lulled into a delusive security, the war parties of the other nations, often joined by the Cayuga warriors, would overwhelm them by a sudden onset. But it was not by their craft, nor by their organization, which for military purposes was wretchedly feeble. It was amazing that the Iroquois could gain such a bloody supremacy. They carried all before them because they were animated throughout, as one man, by the same audacious pride and insatiable rage for conquest.

Like other Native Americans, they waged war on a plan altogether democratic, that is, each man fought or not as he saw fit, and they owed their unity and vigor of action to the homicidal frenzies that urged them all alike.

The Neutral Nation had taken no part, on either side, in the war of extermination against the Huron's, and their towns were sanctuaries where either of the contending parties might take asylum.

On the other hand, they made fierce war on their western neighbors, and, a few years before, destroyed, with atrocious cruelties, a large fortified town of the Nation of Fire. Their turn had now come, and their victims found fit avengers, for no sooner were the Huron's broken up and dispersed than the Iroquois, without waiting to take a breath, turned their fury on the Neutrals.

At the end of the autumn of 1650, they assaulted and took one of their chief towns containing, at the time, more than sixteen hundred men, besides the women and children.

Early the following spring, they took another town. The slaughter was monstrous, and the victors drove back troops of captives for butchery and adoption.

It was a death blow of the Neutrals. They had abandoned their cornfields and villages in the wildest terror, and dispersed themselves abroad in forests, which could not yield sustenance for such a multitude. They perished by the thousands and from that time forth the nation ceased to exist.

During the next three years, the Iroquois contented themselves with harassing the French and Algonquians, but in 1653 they made treaties of peace. In the following May, an Onondaga orator on a peace visit to Ville-Marie, said in a speech to the Governor, "Our young men will no more fight the French; but they are too warlike to stay home, and this summer we shall invade the country of the Eries. The earth trembles and quakes in that quarter, but here all remains calm."

Early in the autumn, Father Le Moyne, who had taken advantage of the peace went on a mission to the Onondagas, returned with the tidings that the Iroquois were all on fire with this new enterprise, and were about to march against the Eries with eighteen hundred warriors.

The occasion of this new war is said to have been as follows: the Eries, who it will be remembered dwelt on the north of the lake named after them, made a treaty of peace with the Seneca's, and in the preceding year had sent a deputation of thirty of their principal men to confirm it.

While they were in the great Seneca town, it happened that one of their warriors was killed in a casual quarrel with an Erie, whereupon his countrymen rose in a fury and murdered the thirty deputies.

Then began a brisk war of reprisals, in which not only the Seneca's but the other Iroquois nations took part. The Eries captured a famous Onondaga chief and were about to burn him, when he succeeded in convincing them of the wisdom of a course of conciliation, and they resolved to give him to the sister of one of the murdered deputies to take the place of her lost brother. The sister, by tribal law, had it in her choice to receive him with a fraternal embrace or to burn him. The sister was absent at the time, but no one doubted that she would choose the gentler alternative.

Accordingly, he was clothed in gay attire and all the town fell to feasting in honor of his adoption. In the midst of the feasting the sister returned. To the amazement of the Erie chiefs, she rejected with indignation their proffer of a new brother, declared that she would be revenged for her loss, and she insisted that the prisoner should be burned. The chiefs outlined to the sister the repercussions for the Erie Nation if they proceeded with the burning. The sister could not be convinced to change her mind.

The unfortunate prisoner was stripped of his festal robes, bound to a stake, and put to death. He warned his tormentors with his last breath that they were not only burning him, but the whole Erie nation. He reminded them that his countrymen would take a fiery vengeance for his fate.

His words proved true. No sooner had the story of his burning spread among the Iroquois than the confederacy resounded with war songs from end to end and the warriors took to the field under their two Great War chiefs.

The warriors embarked in canoes on the lake. At their approach the Eries fell back and withdrew west into the forest. When they were gathered into one body they fortified themselves with palisades and felled trees and awaited the approach of the invaders. By the lowest estimate, the Eries numbered two thousand warriors, besides woman and children. But this was the report of the Iroquois, who were naturally disposed to exaggerate the force of their enemies.

They approached the Erie fort, and two of their chiefs, dressed like Frenchmen, advanced and called on those within to surrender. One of them had lately been baptized by Le Moyne, and he shouted to the Eries that if they did not yield in time, they were all dead men, for the master of life was on the side of the Iroquois.

The Eries answered with yells of derision. "Who is this master of your lives?" they cried, "our hatchets and our right arms are the master of ours." The Iroquois rushed to the assault, but they were met with a shower of poisoned arrows, which killed and wounded many of them and drove the rest back. They waited awhile, and then attacked again with determined energy. This time they carried their bark canoes over their heads like huge shields to protect them from the storm of arrows. Then they planted the canoes upright, and mounting them by the crossbars like ladders, scaled the barricade with such fury that the Eries were thrown into a panic. Those who could escape did so, but the butchery was frightful, and from that day the Eries as a nation didn't exist.

The victors paid the price for their conquest. Their losses were so heavy that they were forced to remain for two months in the Erie country, to bury their dead and nurse their wounded.

One enemy of their own race remained and that enemy was the Andastes. This nation appears to have been inferior in numbers to the Huron's, the Neutrals, or the Eries, but they cost their assailants more trouble than all these united.

The Mohawks seemed at first to have borne the brunt of the Andastes war, and, between the years 1650 and 1660, they were so roughly handled by these stubborn adversaries, that they were reduced from the height of audacious insolence to the depths of dejection.

The remaining four nations of the Iroquois League now took up the quarrel and fared scarcely better than the Mohawks. In the spring 1658, eight hundred of their warriors set out for the Andastes country to strike a decisive blow, but when they reached the great town of their enemies along the shores of the Susquehanna River, they learned that the Andastes had received both aid and counsel from the neighboring Swedish colonists. The town was fortified by a double palisade, flanked by two bastions, on which several small pieces of cannon were mounted. Clearly, it was not to be carried by assault as the invaders had promised themselves. Their only hope was in treachery, and, accordingly, twenty-five of their warriors gained entrance on the pretense of settling the terms of a peace.

Here, again, ensued a grievous disappointment, for the Andastes seized them all, built high scaffolds visible from without, and tortured them to death in sight of their countrymen.

The Seneca's, by far the most numerous of the five nations, now found them attacked in turn, and this time not by a another native tribe, but by disease: smallpox. The French reaped a profit from their misfortunes, for the disheartened Seneca made them overtures of peace and begged that they would settle in their country, teach them to fortify their towns, supply them with arms and ammunition, and bring them the "Black-Robes" to show them the road to Heaven.

The Andastes war became a war of inroads and skirmishes,

under which the weaker party gradually wasted away. Thus, in 1659, a party of twenty Seneca's and forty Cayugas went against the Andastes. They were a considerable distance from one another, the Cayugas being in advance, when the Seneca's were set upon by about sixty young Andastes, of the class known as "Burnt-Knives," or "Soft-Metals," because these warriors had not taken any scalps. Indeed, they were described as mere boys, fifteen or sixteen years of age. They killed one of the Seneca's, captured another, and put the rest to flight, after which, flushed with their victory, they attacked the Cayugas with the utmost fury and routed them completely, killing eight of them and wounding twice that number. It was reported by a Jesuit in the Cayugas town that the war party came home half dead with gashes of knives and hatchets.

"May God preserve the Andastes," exclaimed the Father, "and we and our missions be left in peace!" "None but they," he added elsewhere, "can curb the pride of the Iroquois."

The only strength of the Andastes was in their courage. They were eventually reduced to three hundred fighting men, and about the year of 1675 they were finally overcome by the Seneca. Yet they were not wholly destroyed, for a remnant of this valiant people continued to subsist under the name of the Conestogas.

The bloody triumphs of the Iroquois were complete. They had made solitude and called it peace. All the surrounding nations of their own lineage were conquered and broken up, while the neighboring Algonquian tribes were suffered to exist only on condition of paying a yearly tribute of wampum. The confederacy remained a wedge thrust between the growing colonies of France and England

But what was the state of the conquerors? Their triumphs had cost them dearly. As early as the year 1660, a writer, evidently well-informed, reported that their entire force had been reduced to twenty-two hundred warriors, while these not more than twelve hundred were of the true Iroquois stock. The rest was a medley of adopted prisoners, Huron's, Neutrals, Eries, and the rest from various Algonquian tribes

Still their aggressive spirit was not subdued. These incorrigible warriors pushed their murderous raids to Hudson Bay, Lake Superior, the Mississippi, and the Tennessee River. They were the tyrants of all the intervening wilderness and they remained for more than half a century, a terror and a scourge to the afflicted colonists of New France.

With the fall of the Huron Nation, the best hope for all was the New France mission. They, and the stable and populous communities around them, had been the simple material, from which the Jesuit would have formed his Christian empire in the wilderness, but one by one, these kindred peoples were uprooted and swept away, while the neighboring Algonquians, to whom they had been a safeguard, were resolved with them in common ruin. The land of promise was turned into solitude and desolation.

There was still work at hand. It is true that there were vast regions to explore and countless Native Americans to convert, but these, for the most part, were remote and scattered. In a measure, the occupation of the Jesuits was gone. Some of Jesuits went back to France, while the ones who stayed, about twenty in numbers, were victims to famine, hardship, and the Iroquois.

This closes a wild and bloody act of the great drama of New France. The cause of the failure of the Jesuits is obvious. The guns and tomahawks of the Iroquois were the ruin of their hopes. Could they have curbed or converted those ferocious bands? It is a little less than certain that their dream would have become a reality. Taming the Iroquois was scarcely possible. However, if the Jesuits could have accomplished this miracle their habits of agriculture would have been developed and their instincts of mutual slaughter repressed. The swift decline of the Native American population would have been repressed, and it would have been made through the fur trade, a source of prosperity to New France. Unmolested by Iroquois invasions and fed by a rich commerce, the territory would have put forth a vigorous growth.

New France, true to her far-reaching and adventurous genius, would have occupied the West with traders, settlers, and garrisons, and cut up the virgin wilderness into fiefs, while as yet the colonies of England were but a weak and broken line along the shore of the Atlantic; and when at last the great conflict came, England and Liberty would have been confronted, not by a depleted antagonist, still feeble from exhaustion of a starved and persecuted infancy, but by an athletic champion of the principles of Richelieu and of Loyola.

Liberty may thank the Iroquois that, by their insensate fury, the plans of her adversary were brought to naught and a peril and a woe averted from her future. They ruined the trade, which was the lifeblood for New France: they stopped the current of her arteries, and made all her early years a misery and a terror. It changed her destinies. The contest on this continent between Liberty and Absolutism was never doubtful, but the triumph of the one would have been dearly bought, and the downfall of the other incomplete. Populations formed in the ideas and habits of a feudal monarchy, and controlled by a hierarchy profoundly hostile to freedom or thought would have remained a hindrance and a stumbling-block in the way of that majestic experiment of America eventually developed.

The Jesuits saw their hopes struck down, and their faith, though not shaken, was sorely depleted. The Providence of God seemed in their eyes dark and inexplicable, but, from the standpoint of Liberty, that Providence was clear as the sun at noon.

A great philosopher once said: "Meanwhile, let those who have prevailed yield due honor to the defeated. Their virtues shine amidst the rubbish of error, like diamonds and gold in the gravel of the torrent."

Eight

*T*here had been a brief peace negotiated between the French at Quebec, Ville-Marie, Trois Rivieres and the Mohawks. However, over the weeks it was broken by the warriors who didn't want peace with the French. In time, it became evident that the peace was broken, and the hounds of war were turned loose.

The contagion spread through the entire Mohawk nation, the war songs were sung, and the warriors took the path to New France. The colonists and their more miserable allies woke from their dream of peace to a reality of fear and horror. Again, Ville-Marie and Trois Rivieres were beset with murdering warriors, skulking in the thickets and prowling under cover of night, yet, when it came to blows, displaying courage almost equal to the ferocity that inspired it.

They plundered and burned Fort Richelieu that guarded that river, thus leaving the colony without even the semblance of protection. Before spring opened, all the fighting men of the Mohawks had taken to the warpath, but it was clear that many of them still had little heart for their bloody and perfidious work, for, of these hardy and all-enduring warriors, two-thirds gave out along the way, and returned complaining that the season was too severe. Two hundred or more kept on, divided into several bands.

On Ash Wednesday, the French at Trois Rivieres were at mass in the chapel, when the Iroquois, quietly approaching, plundered two houses close to the fort, containing all the property of the neighboring inhabitants.

They hid their booty, and then went in search of two large parties of Christian Algonquians engaged in a winter hunt. Two Algonquians, whom they had captured, set them on the trail of their brothers. They took up the chase like hounds on the scent of game. Wrapped in furs or blanket-coats, some with gun in hand, some with bows and quivers, and all with hatchets, war-clubs, knives, or swords, strode on snowshoes with bodies half bent through the gray forests and the frozen pine-swamps, among wet, black trunks, along dark ravines and under savage hill-sides, their small, fierce eyes darting quick glances that pierced the farthest recesses of the naked woods.

The hunters followed the track of their prey, and eventually found the bark wigwams of the Algonquian camp. The warriors were absent; none were there but women and children. The Iroquois surrounded the huts and captured all of the shrieking inmates. Then ten of them set out to find the traces of the absent hunters.

They soon met up with the renowned chief of the Algonquians, named Piskaret, returning alone. They recognized him as a fierce warrior and decided to use treachery rather than open attack. They approached him as friends. Piskaret was not aware that the peace between the Mohawks and the Algonquians had been breached. Scarcely had they joined him, when one of the Mohawk warriors ran a sword through his body. They scalped him and returned in triumph to their companions. Eventually, all of the hunters were waylaid, overpowered, killed, or taken prisoner.

Another band of Mohawks had meanwhile pursued the other

party of Algonquians and overtook them on the march. They confiscated their sledges and baggage. They moved from one hunting camp to another. The Algonquians would put up a fight and kill some of their assailants, but within a few moments their resistance would be overcome, and those who managed to survive the fray would be helplessly in the clutches of the enraged victors. They would then begin to massacre the old, the disabled, and the infants, with the usual beating, gashing, and severing of fingers.

The next day, the two bands of Mohawks, each with its troop of captives fast bound, met at an appointed spot on the Lake of St. Peter, and greeted each other with yells of exultation, with which mingled a wail of anguish, as the prisoners of either party recognized their companions in misery. They all knelt in the midst of their savage conquerors, and one of the men, a noted convert, after a few words of exhortation, repeated in a loud voice a prayer, to which the rest responded. Then they sang an Algonquian hymn, while the Iroquois, who at first had stared in wonder, broke into laughter and derision, and at length fell upon them with renewed fury. One was burned alive on the spot. Another attempted to escape, and they burned the soles of his feet that he might not repeat his attempt. Many others were maimed and mangled, and some of the women, who afterward managed to escape, affirmed that, in ridicule of the converts, they crucified a small child by nailing it with wooden spikes against a thick sheet of bark.

The prisoners were led to the Mohawk towns, and it is needless to repeat the monotonous and revolting tale of torture and death. The men as usual were burned, but the lives of the women and children were spared in order to strengthen the conquerors by their adoption. However, the women were made to endure the extremes of suffering and indignity. Several of them from time to time escaped and reached New France with the story of their woes.

Among these was Marie, the wife of Jean Baptiste, one of the principal Algonquian converts, who was captured and burned with the rest. Early in June, she appeared in a canoe at Ville-Marie, where Madame d'Ailleboust, to whom she was well known, received her with great kindness.

Marie has once before been a prisoner of the Iroquois at the town of Onondaga. When she and her companions in misfortune had reached the Mohawk towns, she was recognized by several Onondagas who chanced to be there, and who, partly by threats and partly by promises, induced her to return with them to the scene of her former captivity, where they assured her good treatment. With their aid, she escaped from the Mohawks, and set out with them for Onondaga. On their way, they passed the great town of the Oneidas, and her conductors, fearing that certain Mohawks who were there would lay claim to her, found a hiding place for her in the forest, where they gave her food and told her to wait for their return.

She lay concealed all day, and at night approached the town under the cover of darkness. A dull red glare of flames rose above the jagged tops of the palisade that encompassed it, and, from the pandemonium within, an uproar of screams, yells, and bursts of laughter told her that they were burning one of her captive countrymen.

She gazed and listened, shivering with cold and aghast with horror. The thought possessed her that she would soon share his fate and she resolved to flee. The ground was covered with snow, and her footprints would infallibly have betrayed her if she had not, instead of turning toward home, followed the beaten Indian path westward.

After several miles, she approached the Onondaga, a few miles from the present day city of Syracuse, and hid herself in a dense thicket of spruce or cedar. She crept forth at night to grope in the half-melted snow for a few ears of corn left from the last year's harvest.

She saw many Iroquois from her lurking place, and at once a tall warrior with an axe on his shoulder advanced directly towards the spot where she lay. In the extremity of her fright, she murmured a prayer. Like a miracle, he turned and changed course. She knew that the fate that awaited her if she remained could not hope for mercy. The terrible dangers of the pitiless wilderness, between her and Canada, filled her with despair, for she was half dead already from hunger and cold.

She finally gave in to her despondency. She tied her girdle to the branch of a tree and hung herself from it by the neck. The cord broke. She repeated the attempt with the same result, and then the thought came to her that God meant to save her life.

The snow by this time had melted in the forest and she began her journey for home. Her only provision was a handful of corn. She directed her course by the sun, and for food she dug roots, peeled the soft inter bark of trees, and, at one point, caught tortoises in a muddy brook. She had the good fortune to find a hatchet in a deserted camp and with it made implements she used for kindling a fire. The fire saved her from the worst suffering, since she only had a thin tunic that left her arms and legs bare which exposed her at night to the tortures of the cold.

She built a fire in some deep nook of the forest, warmed herself, and cooked what whatever she found to eat. At daylight, she would throw water on the embers of the fire, so the rising smoke would not attract attention.

Once she came upon a party of Iroquois hunters. She lay concealed and they passed without seeing her. She followed their trail back and she found their bark canoe, which they had hidden near the bank of the river. It was too large for her use, but she was a practiced canoe maker so she reduced it to a convenient size. When the work was completed, she launched the canoe and paddled down the river. The stream connected to the St. Lawrence and she paddled with the current towards Ville-Marie.

On islands and rocky shores she found eggs of waterfowl in abundance; she speared fish with a sharpened pole, hardened at the point with fire. She killed deer by driving them into the water, chasing them in her canoe, and striking them on the head with her hatchet. When she landed at Ville-Marie, her canoe had still a good store of eggs and dried venison.

Her journey from Onondaga had occupied about two months, under hardships which no women but a Native American could survive. Escapes not less remarkable of several other women are chronicled in the records of this same year, and one of them, called for a brief notice.

Eight Algonquians, in one of those fits of desperate valor which sometimes occurred in Native Americans, entered at midnight a camp where thirty Iroquois warriors were buried in sleep, and with quick, sharp blows of their tomahawks began to brain them as they lay. They killed ten of them on the spot and wounded many more. The rest, panic-stricken and bewildered by the surprise, in the darkness fled into the forest, leaving all they had in the hands of the victors, including a number of Algonquian captives, of whom one had been unwittingly killed by his countrymen in the confusion.

Another captive of the Iroquois, a woman, had escaped on a previous night. They had stretched her on her back, with limbs extended, and bound her wrists and ankles to four stakes firmly driven into the earth, their ordinary mode of securing prisoners. Then, as usual, they all fell asleep. She presently became aware that the cord that bound one of her wrists was somewhat loose, and, by long and painful efforts, she freed her hand. To release the other hand and her feet was then comparatively easy.

She cautiously rose. Around her, breathing in deep sleep, laid stretched the dark forms of the unconscious warriors, scarcely visible in the gloom. She stepped over them to the entrance of the hut, and here, as she was passing out, she discovered a hatchet on the ground. The temptation was too strong for her Algonquian nature. She seized it, and struck again and again, with all her force, on the skull of the Iroquois who lay at the entrance. The sounds of the blows and the convulsive struggling of the victim roused the sleepers. They sprung up, groping in the dark, demanding of each other what was the matter.

Eventually, they lighted a roll of birch-bark and found their prisoner gone and their comrade dead. They rushed out in search of the fugitive. She meanwhile, instead of running away, had hid herself in the hollow of a tree, which she had observed the evening before.

Her pursuers ran through the dark woods, shouting to each other, and when all the Iroquois had passed, she crept from her hiding place and fled in an opposite direction. In the morning, they found her tracks and followed them.

On the second day they had overtaken and surrounded her, when hearing their cries on all sides, she gave up all hope. But at the last minute she noticed in the thickest depths of the forest that the beavers had damned a brook and formed a pond, full of gnawed stumps, dead fallen trees, rank weeds, and tangled bushes. She plunged in, and, swimming and wading, found a hiding place, where her body was concealed by the water and her head by the masses of dead and living vegetation. Her pursuers after a long search gave up the chase in despair.

Shivering, naked, and half-starved, she crawled out from her hiding place and resumed her flight. By day, the briers and bushes tore her unprotected limbs; by night, she shivered with cold. The mosquitoes and small black gnats of the forest persecuted her. She subsisted on such roots, bark, reptiles, and other small animals as her knowledge of the forest enabled her to gather along the way.

She crossed streams by swimming or on rafts of driftwood, lashed together with strips of linden-bark, and at length reached the St. Lawrence, where, with the aid of her hatchet, she made a canoe. Her home was on the Ottawa, and she was ignorant of the St. Lawrence, or at least this part of it.

She had scarcely even seen a Frenchman, but had heard of the French as friends, and she knew that they had dwellings along the banks of the St. Lawrence. This was her only guide, and she drifted on her way, doubtful whether the vast current would bear her to the abodes of the living.

Passing the watery wilderness of the Lake of St. Peter she spotted a Huron canoe. Fearing that it was the enemy, she hid herself and resumed her voyage in the evening. Soon she came upon the wooden buildings and palisades of Trois Rivieres. Several Huron's saw her at the same moment and made their way toward her. When her canoe reached the shore, she leaped onto the shore and hid in the bushes. Since she was naked, she would not come out until they provided her with some clothing.

After she was dressed in her new clothes, she went with them to the fort and the house of the Jesuits. She was in a wretched state of emaciation, but was in high spirits. She was grateful to be among friends.

Such stories might be multiplied, but these will suffice. Nor is it necessary to dwell further on the bloody record of butcheries and tortures. We have seen enough to show the nature of the scourge that now fell without mercy on the Indians and French of New France. There was no safety but the imprisonment of palisades and ramparts. A deep dejection fell over the white and red men alike of New France.

Nine

*I*n the late summer of 1658, four weeks after Adam arrived at Ville-Marie, a dozen canoes and a small barge arrived with supplies from Quebec. Two of the main items were thirty new harquebusiers and twenty-five casks of gun powder.

When Adam began the training of the men of the fortress, he was appalled at the condition and age of the harquebusiers that were being carried for protection against the Iroquois. Although the Iroquois had harquebusiers that they had received from trading fur to the Dutch at Fort Orange, the majority of the five Iroquois nations still used their bow and arrows with extreme accuracy.

The new harquebusiers were disturbed to the men of the fort. They were also reminded that an Iroquois could fire ten arrows within the time a militiaman could reload his weapon. Therefore, it was very important that when taking aim with their weapons, they waited for the enemy to be in as close range as possible without taking a hit by one of their arrows.

Adam had the carpenters of the fort make a number of longbows and a thousand arrows. In France, the army used the longbow in battle and used the harquebusiers as a backup weapon. Adam's mission was to train these men at Ville-Marie like the soldiers of France were prepared for war. The longbow delivered an arrow accurately and carried twice the distance the bows the Iroquois employed.

Targets were set up at the parade field and practice with the longbow was conducted in the mornings. In the afternoon, the men fired the harquebusiers in formation. In other words, when the man in front fired his weapon, he would move to the rear of the column and reload, which took about three minutes; the second man found a target and fired, and in turn moved to the rear of the column. They would continue this rotation through three columns until Adam declared a "ceasefire."

This intensive training was conducted every other day. Since the men had work to do in their fields, they were incapable of having the training every day. Adam had the men divided into two platoons; that way there was always training being conducted.

As the harvest season was approaching, Adam conferred with Le Moyne, who was very familiar with the ambush techniques of the Iroquois and many of their hiding places. Adam believed that it was time to rout the Iroquois from the island, so he and Le Moyne developed systematic plan to rid the island of the Iroquois once and for all.

The Iroquois were very superstitious. They believed that a spirit, through a dead individual, sent them a warning. Le Moyne and Adam decided to decapitate all the Iroquois they killed and place their heads on poles at various distances around the island. The purpose of placing these heads was when a canoe of Iroquois would come ashore, they would take note of the heads of these fallen comrades and get the message that this too could happen to them. Adam believed that placing these decapitated heads along the Prairies River at various intervals would also act as a repellent and discourage the warriors from coming onto the island.

Adam spent a month drilling the men on such harquebus commands as "prime and load," "open pan," "handle cartridge," "prime," "about," "draw ramrods," "ram down cartridge," "return rammers," "make ready," "present," and "fire!" This process was drilled into the troops until they could complete the procedure upon hearing a single command of "prime and load." The purpose of this training was to have the militiamen able to load and fire a round per minute, rather than the three minutes it normally took in the past.

All the men were trained on the longbow. The ones that excelled at longbow practice would engage the enemy while a partner would reload his harquebus. The ranks were broken down in groups of three, two with harquebusiers and one with a longbow.

One day, while the men were training, a flotilla of Iroquois appeared in front of Ville-Marie. They stood up in their canoes, shouted obscenities and made threatening gestures. The men that were training at the time, rushed to the walls to observe this Iroquois performance.

When Adam observed these Iroquois gyrations, he became furious and was determined to respond. He had one of the cannons on the wall loaded and primed. In the lead canoe was an Iroquois chief identified by his headdress. Adam had the cannon aimed at the chief's canoe. On Adam's command the cannon was fired, and the chief's canoe received a direct hit killing or wounding the six Iroquois in the canoe. The chief was knocked out of the canoe, and although slightly injured, he began to swim to another canoe to be rescued. Adam took a primed harquebus from one of the militiamen standing next to him and got a beat on the chief. He fired hitting his target in the head removing part of his skull. His fellow warriors lifted his body into a canoe and they continued their journey up the St. Lawrence River toward the Ottawa River.

The Iroquois learned a lesson not to flaunt themselves in front of Ville-Marie within cannon and gun range.

A few days after the Iroquois appeared in front of Ville-Marie, Adam believed it was time to rid the island of this Iroquois infestation. He met with Le Moyne after the training one evening to discuss a plan. Le Moyne laid out a crude map of the island and briefed Adam where he believed they usually came ashore, and the areas where he believed they were camped. He said that rather than attempting to ambush them by land, it might be more practical to attack them by water.

After it got dark, Le Moyne took Adam up on the ramparts and showed him the Iroquois fires that were burning at their various camp sites. "They are confident that we won't come out of our fortress at night in fear of getting attacked. As you can see we can identify their locations and we can easily attack them from the water. It will be the element of surprise that will overwhelm them. We'll use the longbows as our weapons of choice."

Le Moyne and Adam took note of the several fires burning across the island and made notations on the Le Moyne map. They decided to select the Iroquois site closest to the fort. The plan was to silently attack, kill all the occupants and place their heads on polls along the river.

The very next day, Adam spent several hours of longbow training with his recruits. Two of the men showed exceptional skill using the weapon. One of them, Alonie Delestre, had served in the army in France and had previously been taught in the use of the longbow. He was able to fire, accurately, seven arrows a minute which was exceptional. Jean Valets was also impressive with hitting five bull's-eyes.

Along with the two archers, Adam selected three other militia-men for the attack on the Iroquois camp later in the week. The plan was to silently kill the Iroquois camped at the far end of the island, decapitate them, and plant their heads at suspected landing areas around the island. This was going to be a three-night operation, using all the militiamen for the two nights after killing all or most of the Iroquois and circumnavigate the island.

On Friday that October night around the midnight hour, Adam, Le Moyne, and the five militiamen assembled at the front gate of the fort. They carried their canoes out to the pier and launched the craft. In their possession were knives, hatches, longbows, and arrows along with harquebusiers. They shoved off in the downriver direction keeping close to the shoreline.

It was very dark, but Le Moyne knew the way and he was in the lead canoe. Their destination was the tip of the island at the St. Lawrence and the Prairies Rivers confluence. Le Moyne had told Adam he believed that the Iroquois came ashore along the Prairies River. As they turned into the Prairies River the smoke from one of their encampments could be detected.

Silently, they paddled down the river until they saw a small fire burning in the distance. They beached the canoes and cautiously made their way through the woods. As they came to an open area, one of the militiamen saw a figure leaning against a tree. Le Moyne believed that he was the Iroquois lookout. Both of the longbow men were brought forward and instructed to take aim. On Le Moyne's order they let loose with their deadly arrows. One arrow pierced the Iroquois' throat and the second arrow was a direct hit into his heart. He made a gargling sound and fell to the ground. There were about five figures lying around the fire on blankets. Each militiaman took a target and moved in for the kill. On a silent count of five using his fingers, Adam directed them to kill their target with their hatchets when his last finger disappeared.

Once this party of Iroquois was killed, the French went about the grizzly task of removing the heads of the dead Native Americans. The heads were put into a bag, except for one, and taken back to the canoes. The head was impaled on a pole made from a tree branch and placed at the shoreline where it was believed this war party landed.

Adam, Le Moyne, and the rest of the party took to the canoes and paddled on down the river. They would stop at various distances and place a head on a pole at the shoreline. They continued this practice nearly all the way down the river to where the Prairies River once again connected with the St. Lawrence. Once this planned task was completed, they turned the canoes, paddled back up the Prairies River until it reached the St. Lawrence and back to Ville-Marie.

Adam and Le Moyne went immediately to the governor's quarters and briefed him. The governor was elated with their report and told them to keep up the good work. Adam and Le Moyne agreed that they would repeat similar missions until no more Iroquois fires were detected on the island. As a matter of practice in the future, they intended to walk the ramparts nightly. After spending nearly a half hour going over the night's activity, they retired to their respective quarters.

The following night Adam led fifty of the militia from the fortress across the island in the direction of the Iroquois fires along the Prairies River. Simultaneously, Le Moyne commanded another fifty men in boats and entered the Prairies River from the St. Lawrence. They moved slowly down the river to where an Iroquois fire could be seen. He waited until Adam's men engaged them. Le Moyne's men left their boats and moved on foot to meet the Iroquois in the rear. Adam and Le Moyne formed a pincer movement and killed every one of the Iroquois within their camp. They repeated this tactic every night until the end of the week.

On Saturday, Adam and Le Moyne led about one hundred militia in a long line and swept across the island from its tip to where its mountain raises up at the western end. A few straggling Iroquois were located and eradicated.

Over the next week, Adam and Le Moyne observed that the fires were no longer visible along the shoreline of the Prairies River or anywhere else for that matter. They concluded that their mission the week before was successful.

However, Le Moyne reminded Adam that no burning fires at night could be a ruse. It was his experience that the Iroquois could lie in one position for hours, even days, in the coldest weather to perpetrate an ambush. Le Moyne said, "We cannot let our guard down for a minute. We must continue to provide guards for the farmers as they work in the fields."

The governor rewarded the two men in different ways. He commissioned Le Moyne to the rank of Lieutenant in the militia. Adam was given a piece of land comprising thirty arpents (thirty acres) to farm.

The next two weeks Adam led search parties during the day from one end of the island to the other in search of Iroquois. In two incidents several Iroquois were discovered and eliminated. Adam declared to the governor that in his opinion the island was now free of Iroquois occupation. He assigned several men to squads whose responsibility it was for a quadrant of the island and to assure that it was Iroquois-free. This practice removed the majority of the Iroquois threat and for the most part the farmers could work without being molested or murdered.

The autumn of the year was short. The first snow fell over Ville-Marie at the end of October and continued every few days through November and December. This was Adam's first year in New France and he wasn't acclimated to this freezing climate.

He continued training his militia even on days when the snow piled up to the men's knees. A few of the men told Adam that the Iroquois always left the island in the fall of the year and paddled up the Ottawa to a Great Lake. Once there, they trapped for fur during the winter months and didn't return until spring.

Le Moyne said, "The Iroquois need furs and can no longer find any in their own territories. Consequently, they are forced to hunt in the northern regions of the Ottawa and in the area around the Great Lakes. Generally they spend the winters there, returning down the Ottawa in the spring."

The winter gave way to spring and there was no sign of Iroquois on the island of Ville-Marie. Periodically, however, they would see canoes of Iroquois coming down the Ottawa and crossing in front of the fort along the St. Lawrence with their canoes loaded down with beaver pelts. The Iroquois would always ensure that they stayed out of the range of the fort's artillery.

All spring, Le Moyne and Adam walked the ramparts nightly looking for Iroquois fires, but none were detected.

In the early summer, the Jesuit of Ville-Marie, Pere Joseph Bressani would spend an hour or two walking outside the fort enclosure to say his daily prayers. The population of Ville-Marie was convinced that the Iroquois were no longer on the Island.

That evening when Pere Bressani failed to return, Adam, Le Moyne, and thirty militia soldiers began a thorough search of the area where he was known to walk while saying his prayers. A half-mile from the fort, one of the soldiers found his prayer book lying on the ground. Several feet further, the hat he always wore to protect him from the summer sun was also found. Adam and Le Moyne agreed that his disappearance could only mean one thing: he had fallen into the hands of the Iroquois.

The following spring, a Huron came to Ville-Marie with news of Pere Bressani. He saw the Pere at Fort Orange and Bressani was in deplorable condition. The following account was reported in Bressani's own writing and carried to the fort by the Huron.

The letter is dated the Fifteenth of July from Iroquois country. The letter was soiled and ill-written because he only had one finger on his right hand and could not prevent the blood from his wounds, which were still open, from staining the paper. His ink was gunpowder mixed with water, and his table was the earth.

15 July 1659
Paul de Chomedey de Maisonneuve
Governor, Ville-Marie, New France

Shortly after I was captured, my captors thanked the sun for allowing them to capture me. They took me in a canoe down the St. Lawrence River to the River Richelieu as far as the rapids of Chambly, where we pursued a march on foot among the brambles, rocks, and swamps of a trackless forest. When we reached Lake Champlain, they made new canoes and re-embarked. They landed at its southern extremity six days afterwards and then made for the Upper Hudson. Here they found a fishing camp of four hundred more Iroquois. It was here where my torments began in earnest. They split my hand with a knife, between the little and the ring fingers, and then they beat me with sticks until I was covered in blood. Sometime later, they placed me on a torture-scaffold of bark and presented me to the crowd. They stripped off my clothes and forced me to sing. After about two hours they gave me up to the children. One of them ordered me to dance, at the same time thrusting sharpened sticks into my body and pulling at my hair and beard. "Sing," one would cry. "Hold your tongue!" screamed another; if I obeyed the first, the second one would burn me. "We will burn you to death; we will eat you." "I will eat one of your hands." "And I will eat one of your feet." These scenes were renewed every night for a week.

Every evening a chief cried aloud through the camp, "Come, my children, come and caress our prisoners!" A large crowd thronged jubilant to a large hut, where the captives lay. They stripped off the fragment of my cassock which was my only garment and then they proceeded to burn me with live coals and red-hot stones. I was forced to walk on hot cinders. They burned off a fingernail and then the joint of a finger. They rarely proceeded with more than one torture, since they wanted to economize their pleasures, and reserve the rest for another day. The torture of the prisoners was protracted till one or two o'clock in the morning, after which they left me on the ground, fast bound to four stakes, and covered only with a scanty fragment of deerskin. The other prisoners had their share of torture. There was a young boy about twelve or thirteen years old and he was tormented before me with pitiless ferocity.

After several days in this encampment, and after another march of several days, during which I spent wading in a rocky stream, I fell from exhaustion and was nearly drown. When we finally reached the next town, I was hung by the feet with chains; they placed food for their dogs on my body that they might lacerate me as they ate. I became so emaciated that even they seemed to stand in horror of me. I could not believe that a man was so hard to kill.

They suddenly stopped the torture and began to feed me. They told me in jest that they wished to fatten me before putting me to death. Eventually, a council met to decide my fate and to my surprise they resolved to spare my life. I was given to an old woman to take the place of a deceased relative, but she was repulsed at my mangled condition, *as by the Indian standard, I was useless. She had her son take me to Fort Orange and sell me to the Dutch.*

The Dutch gave a generous ransom for me, supplied me with clothing and kept me until I restored my strength. I am about to embark onboard a vessel bound for Rochelle. I am giving this letter to a friendly Huron to carry to Ville-Marie in order to inform my parish there as to my trials and tribulations. It is my sincere hope that once my health is restored, I shall return to New France and continue my work there. God bless all of you.

Pere, Joseph Bressani, SJ

In October at Quebec, a party of French Algonquin's captured a Wolf, or Mohegan Indian, that had been naturalized among the Iroquois and brought him to that city. They burned him there with their usual atrocity of torture. Two Jesuits attempted to save him, but their attempts were in vain. Although, the Jesuits were just halfheartedly attempting to save the Mohegan's life, since they believed that torture seemed to be a blessing in disguise. They thought that it was good for the soul, and in the case of obduracy, the surest way to salvation. "We have rarely indeed," wrote one of them, "seen the burning of an Iroquois without feeling sure that he was on the path to Paradise; and we never knew one of them to be surely on the path to Paradise without seeing him pass through this fiery punishment."

So they let the Wolf burn, but first, having instructed him after their fashion, they baptized him, and his savage soul flew to heaven out of the fire. "It is not," pursued the same writer, "a marvel to see a wolf changed at one stroke into a lamb, and enter the fold of Christ which he came to ravage?"

Before the Mohegan died, he informed the French that there were eight hundred Iroquois warriors encamped below Ville-

Marie and that four hundred more, who had wintered on the Ottawa, were on the point of joining them. This army would swoop down on Quebec, lay waste to the city, kill the governor, and then attack Trois Rivieres and Ville-Marie.

It was believed by the French that this time the Iroquois were in dead earnest. The City of Quebec was in a wild terror. The Ursuline's and the nuns of the Hotel Dieu took refuge in the strong and extensive building which the Jesuits had just completed opposite the Parish Church. Its walls and palisades made it easy of defense, and in its yards and court were lodged the terrified Huron's, as well as the fugitive inhabitants of the neighboring settlements. Others found asylum in the fort, and still others in the Convent of the Ursuline's, which, in place of nuns, was occupied by twenty-four soldiers, who fortified it with redoubts, and barricaded the doors and windows.

Similar measures of defense were taken at the Hotel Dieu, and the streets of the Lower Town were strongly barricaded. Everybody was in arms, and the "Qui vive" of the sentries and patrols resounded all night. Meanwhile, two young Frenchmen and two Algonquin boarded a canoe and paddled up the St. Lawrence. Their first stop was Trois Rivieres, and then it was on to Ville-Marie to inform them of the Iroquois Army that was reported forming down the Richelieu River.

During one evening in mid-December, while Le Moyne and Adam walked the ramparts, the conversation turned to the Iroquois wintering up north and coming down the Ottawa River in the spring with the furs they trapped that season. It was during that conversation when Adam conceived the idea of ambushing the Iroquois on their way back down the Ottawa River and relieving them of their bounty.

Ten

*O*n Christmas Eve, the entire colony attended mass with the exception of the few guards on duty that walked the ramparts. Adam and Le Moyne were invited to share the pew with the governor and his family. Afterwards, the governor extended an invitation to join him to celebrate the holiday at his quarters. There was a sumptuous feast laid out on a long table and several musicians had been employed to provide music. The few ladies of the colony were also invited to provide partners for the male guests to dance.

It became obvious as the evening wore on that the governor's daughter, Bernadette, had become smitten with Adam. He enjoyed the attention being displayed and they danced most of the night. Adam was beginning to have romantic feelings for this young, beautiful woman. Something inside of him, however, resisted these feelings. He kept referring back to his experiences in France, and how that had ruined his military career and brought him to this cold, dark, remote wilderness where death was behind every tree. Although he was as smitten with Bernadette as she appeared to be with him, he had to keep his feelings in check. At the end of the evening, he thanked the governor and Bernadette for a wonderful evening, bid them a good night and walked through the snow back to his quarters.

As Adam entered his cabin, he was feeling very melancholy. He sat down at the table and lit a candle. It was early on Christmas morning. His thoughts were thousands of miles away thinking of his beloved Geruese. He sat there for several minutes staring at the candle flame becoming almost hypnotized. He wondered what she was doing at that very moment. He was having regrets for not meeting with Marguerite that afternoon before he left Paris and learning what the message was from Geruese. She may have had a plan to escape from that Convent where she was being held against her will. He could have helped her in an escape. Then he could have hid her until she turned eighteen and had reached the age of consent. They could have married.

He finally came to his senses and realized that fantasizing about what he should have done was not going to change the past. He was in New France now; he was Adam Dollard and not Adam Daulac, and he was cold as hell.

After a few minutes, he opened one of the last bottles of wine that he had brought from France, poured a full glass, drank it straight down, and poured another. Sitting there in the candlelight, he finished the rest of the bottle. It was time to go to bed. He had a long day ahead of him the next day training his little army.

Changing into his night shirt, he lost no time climbing under the blankets. His little cabin was freezing. Within minutes, he was sound asleep.

After what seemed like hours, but couldn't have been more than a few minutes, Adam suddenly awakened. As his eyes became accustomed to the dark, he saw a figure standing alongside his bed looking down at him. He reached for his flintlock pistol that he always kept loaded on a table next to the bed. He stopped in his tracks when a voice he knew said his name.

"Adam, it's me, Bernadette."

His heart was beating out of his chest. He looked up at her and said, "Bernadette, what are you doing here?" He took another pause. "Does your father know that you're here?"

She sat on the side of the bed and ignored his question concerning her father. "I could feel your body reacting to me when you held me tightly while dancing this evening. I know that you are attracted to me and it would be foolish for us not to be together."

Adam looked at her with an excitement that he hadn't experienced since he was alone with Geruese many months ago back in Paris.

"It's very cold in here. May I join you under those blankets?"

Before Adam could object, she opened her coat and it dropped on the floor. She was completely naked. She pulled back the blankets as she said, "Move over, I'm freezing."

Adam did as she requested, but he lay completely still, almost afraid to move. The bed was small and their bodies were touching. Seconds passed when he inquired, "What would your father say if he learned that you came here?"

She didn't respond to his question as she turned on her side and faced him. "I knew from the first time we met that I would give my body to you eventually. As we were dancing tonight at the Christmas gathering, it became clear that tonight would be the night for us to make love for the first time."

Adam turned on his side facing her. Her body was pressed against his and he could feel his blood pressure rising.

She let her hand touch his full erection. "I can see that you want me as well." She took a short pause before she said, "You don't know how lonely I've been cooped up in this little fort all these years. I have needs, and when I've been in close proximity to you, I can detect that you have similar needs as well." She took another pause, and then she said, "If you don't kiss me, I think I'll scream."

He put his right arm behind her head and pulled her body even more tightly toward him as their lips touched. The kiss was long and passionate. Together, they explored each other's bodies with their free hands.

Adam, for all practical purposes, was a worldly man, but he was raised in a very strict orthodox Catholic environment that did not approve of sex before marriage. There was more than one occasion when he entertained sexual thoughts about Geruese, but he never dreamed of acting on them. Now, here he was on this cold night in Ville-Marie, thousands of miles from Paris, in bed with a beautiful young woman wanting him to ravish her. He began to let himself go. She wanted this to happen, so he gave in to his better judgement. He began to kiss and explore her entire body to her delight. Her breathing became heavy and labored. She encouraged him to explore. He was doing things to Bernadette that he only dreamed of doing to a woman throughout his puberty. He kissed and licked every inch of her body. She had opened her legs wide to allow him entrance. Before he made the final move he asked, "Have you made any provisions for birth control. You don't want to have a baby in this godforsaken place."

The passion was momentarily broken. She was finding it somewhat difficult to talk about this subject, but she knew it had to be discussed. She paused and then she said, "There was a Huron woman who lived with her husband at the fort about a year ago. She had two small children about a year apart. One day she confided to me that she didn't want any more children because her husband was having difficulty providing for the two they already had. I asked her how she could make that decision without some kind of help. She showed me a root that she ingested every day that prevented her from becoming pregnant. Until you arrived at Ville-Marie, I didn't have a need to ingest the root. All of the men that live within the walls of this little fort are either married or beneath my social status. The first time I laid my eyes on you, I knew that the time would come when we would be together like we are tonight."

Adam paused to ponder everything Bernadette had just shared with him. He carefully selecting his words as he said, "Bernadette, I find you a very attractive young woman and it would be easy for me to pledge myself to you. But, in fairness, I want you to know that I still have thoughts about a young woman that I left back in Paris. That situation terminated when I left France and came here to begin a new life."

"Were you in love with the woman you left back in Paris?" she prodded.

"Our relationship was reckless and our actions very foolish. It destroyed any chance we could have had for a life together." He turned into her as he said, "I am developing very strong feelings for you. But you're coming here in the middle of the night has a certain amount of adventure to it, but, it can also be very dangerous as well."

There was a long pause in the conversation. "I was very careful leaving the house this evening and I ensured that everyone was fast asleep. When I leave here later, I'll return to my room without anyone realizing I had been absent." She took another short pause. "I promise that I'll be very careful."

Adam countered. "I think that the honorable thing to do is for me to speak with your father and inform him that I am interested in courting his daughter. I have a good rapport with him in other matters."

She took a moment to think over what he just said. "I think

you should wait for a time before you approach my father asking for permission to court me. If my father realizes that you are having feelings for me, he will begin to watch me more carefully. That could prevent me from slipping out at night and coming here."

Adam leaned in and kissed her. "We can take it one day at a time. Maybe you're right. I should spend more time here getting established. That way your father will be more receptive to my request to court you."

They made love for the next hour. Afterwards, they held each other in a tight embrace for several minutes. Bernadette broke the silence. "I should go now. I'll plan on coming back tomorrow about the same time."

They kissed again before separating. Once out of bed she picked up her coat from the floor, put it on, and exited out the door and into the dark night.

For the rest of the month (December) she came to Adam every night.

On New Year's Eve Adam waited up for her arrival. Around one o'clock the door opened and she entered. Adam invited her to sit down at the table and he poured her a glass of wine. They sat looking at each other over the flickering candle flame. Seconds passed when Adam said, "We can't continue this liaison. I'm afraid your father is going to discover what we've been doing and punish both of us. I intend to approach him in the near future and ask for your hand in marriage. I love you and want to be with you, but we have to do this the proper way."

"When will you speak with him?" she inquired.

"As soon as the time is right, and when I secure this little fort from the grip of the Iroquois. At that time, your father will owe me his gratitude and will welcome me as a son-in-law."

They continued to sit quietly for several minutes drinking their wine. Eventually, Bernadette suggested they go to bed for the last time until she became his bride.

Adam agreed. They moved toward the bed and undressed. He took her into his arms and they kissed. Adam removed the blankets and Bernadette slipped within as Adam followed. They made love until almost dawn.

Eleven

B y the time January was exhausted on the calendar, Adam didn't think that he would ever thaw out. This was his second winter in Ville-Marie and he still had not acclimated. His men were ready, in his opinion, for a military engagement. He discussed the possibility of engaging the Iroquois on their return trip down the Ottawa River to relieve them of their furs that they had spent the winter trapping.

It was about that time, too, when two Algonquin arrived at Ville-Marie and informed the governor that the Iroquois were proposing that the entire five nations send all of their warriors to the islands of the Richelieu River for the purpose of destroying every last French person in New France. Adam and Le Moyne knew some kind of action had to be recommended to confront this army of Iroquois. They spent two days constructing a plan to be presented to the governor.

On the third day, with a plan in hand, Le Moyne and Adam walked to the governor's quarters and requested a meeting. "Sir," Le Moyne said, "If we don't do something to deter the Iroquois, they will appear around our little settlement in the late spring and overwhelm us."

The governor shook his head in agreement. Le Moyne continued, "Monsieur Dollard and I have developed a plan to make the Iroquois rethink their plan to attack the colonies of

New France, and injure them to the point that they will return back to their villages with their tails between their legs."

For several moments the governor didn't respond. The governor appeared to be simultaneously worried and interested in their plan.

"Governor, is everything all right?" Le Moyne inquired.

"I'm listening," the governor said, "continue."

Adam put the written plan on the table. "Excellency, the plan is a very simple one. We recruit volunteers from the Ville-Marie colony, take as many arms and supplies as we can physically carry, and go up the Ottawa River. When the Iroquois come down from their winter hunting, attack them and take their furs. Meanwhile, a few of us will return with the fur bounty and the rest of us will remain on the Ottawa. We will allow a few of the Iroquois to escape and come down the river to inform their army that is forming at the Richelieu River. This will invoke their fury, and hopefully they will change their mission of attacking the French colonies to attacking us on the Ottawa."

"Will both of you head this expedition?" the governor asked.

"No," Adam said. "Lieutenant Le Moyne will remain here in the event that our plan fails and the Iroquois attack Ville-Marie."

"How did you reach a decision as to which one of you will lead the expedition up the Ottawa?" the governor inquired.

Le Moyne smiled and said, "We flipped a coin and I lost."

The two men shook hands with the governor. "Sir, there is another private personal matter I would like to discuss with you," Adam injected.

Le Moyne bowed to the governor; he turned and left the room.

After a moment, Adam began, "Sir, your daughter, Bernadette, is a beautiful and refined young woman. Since I arrived at Ville-Marie the relationship between your daughter and me has evolved from friendship to a physical, spiritual, and emotional one. We have professed our love for one another and I informed her recently that the honorable thing to do was to ask for her hand in the holy institution of marriage. I realize the military mission that I am about to embark is very dangerous and there is a good possibility that I may not return."

A troubled looked passed over the governor's face.

Adam continued, "Sir, your daughter's happiness is very important to me. Therefore, in the time I have left before going up the Ottawa to meet our enemy, I want everyone to know that Bernadette and I are in love and we want to eventually be together."

Adam took a cautious pause before he said, "Sir, therefore, I humbly and formally ask for your daughter's hand in holy marriage."

The governor was silent for several seconds. "Colonel, you are about to embark on a very dangerous mission. I will pray every day that you and the other young brave men of Ville-Marie, who will be accompanying you, return to this fort safely and successful. But before I bless your request, I would like my daughter, Bernadette, to stand by your side and listen to what I have to say."

The door adjacent to the meeting room had been ajar during this whole conversation between the governor and Adam. The door opened completely and Bernadette entered the room. She took her place alongside Adam, facing her father. "I am here at Adam's side to hear what it is you have to say, Father." She put her arm into Adam's arm and looked into her father's eyes.

"I just have a few questions. First, Colonel Dollard, presuming you return from this dangerous mission and marry my daughter, how do you propose to support her? Your current financial means will not allow her to live in a custom she has been raised."

Bernadette spoke up to answer her father's concern. "It's true; we haven't discussed the practical side of this proposed union. I just know that no matter what Adam decides in the future to provide means for our family; it will be fully acceptable to me."

"That is a romantic attitude, dear child, but I am afraid it is not a very realistic one."

"Sir, if and when I return from the Ottawa River, I will write to my brother who inherited the family estate and impose upon him to offer me a position. I am quite sure that with a letter from you outlining my service to Ville-Marie and New France, he will be more than eager allow me to partner with him. Bernadette will become an important part of our family and she will be company for my young sister who resides on the estate."

Turning to Bernadette the governor asked a hypothetical question: "And if Adam doesn't return from his mission, will you continue with your former plans to move to Quebec and teach at the school for a period of time before returning to Paris?"

"If Adam doesn't return, I couldn't remain here with my memories. I will follow my previous plan to go to Quebec," she responded with a touch of sadness in her voice.

The governor took a moment to collect his thoughts and then he said, "Please take each other's hand and hold them up so I can lay my hand over the both of yours."

He placed his hand over theirs and spoke. Looking directly at Adam, "I couldn't ask for a more honest and brave son." He turned back to both of them, "My daughter has made her decision to marry you from her heart, and therefore, it is my honor to bless your request to become engaged to be married when you return from the Ottawa."

"Thank you, sir, you won't regret your decision, I promise."

Bernadette moved to her father and embraced him. "Thank you, Father, for your blessing. Adam will make a proud addition to our family."

After taking a long pause to look at Adam and Bernadette, he said, "I shall make an announcement about the engagement and we shall have a dinner to celebrate this proposed union." He turned and left the room.

Adam leaned in and kissed Bernadette. "I have to leave you now, I have duties to perform. He kissed her again and left the mansion to begin recruiting young men to volunteer for the mission in the spring.

Over the next few days they managed to enlist the following men: Jacques Brassier, Francois Crussion Pilote, Rene Doussin, Nicolas Josselin, Nicolas Josselin, Jean Lecompte, Etienne Robin, Jean Tavernier de La Forest, Jean Valets, Christophe Augier Desjardins, Jacques Boisseau, Alone Delestre, Simon Grenet, Roland Hebert, Robert Jurie, Louis Martin and Nicolas Tiblemont.

All of these men went into training under Adam to learn to art of hand-to-hand combat. They were especially briefed in the use of a knife and hatchet in close quarters. Finally, they were schooled on making and delivering explosives made from gun powder.

Everything else in Adam's life became a low priority. He was intent on engaging the Iroquois with the most intense war he had at his disposal. Le Moyne attended these classes from time to time, but wasn't allowed to participate. Time was too short to allow someone who was not going to be at the Long Sault to take time away from militiamen who were going into combat.

A few days later, Adam received a written invitation to attend that evening his engagement dinner at the governor's mansion. Bernadette and he were going to be the guests of honor. When he got home from the training, he took a shower as best he could, washed his hair, and put on his finest clothes.

As he walked toward the mansion, the door opened and Bernadette was standing in the doorway to welcome him. He slowly walked up the front stairs, took her into his arms, and kissed her passionately. When they moved away from each other Adam said, "Good evening, my future wife."

Bernadette responded, "And a pleasant evening to you, my intended husband." Hand in hand they entered the mansion and she led him into the dining hall. All of the important residents of Ville-Marie were present to congratulate them.

The governor was the last to enter. He walked up to the head of the table and invited everyone to have a seat. A servant moved around the table and poured a glass of very expensive wine from Paris into each of the guest's glasses.

After everyone had been accommodated, the governor raised his glass and made a toast. "I have decided to have my precious, one and only child given in marriage to Colonel Adam Dollard. It is my sincere hope that they live happily ever after and give me many grandchildren. Everyone, let's have an applause for Adam and Bernadette."

Everyone clapped their hands loudly and then responded, "To Adam and Bernadette!" as they raised their wine glasses in the fashion of a toast.

The governor took a sip of his wine and implored everyone to enjoy the meal.

There was light conversation and congratulations throughout the evening. A string quartet played some romantic music, and on several occasions Adam and Bernadette danced romantically to the French melodies of the time.

When the evening finally ended, all the guests began to leave one at a time. Finally, there was just the governor, Adam, and Bernadette remaining. They both thanked the governor for a lovely evening. He left the room, leaving them alone to say goodnight.

Adam took her into his arms and they kissed passionately.

Bernadette whispered to Adam, "It's taking every bit of discipline I have not to come to your cottage later this evening."

"We have to behave honorably throughout this engagement. I love you and want to be with you as well, but we can't do anything that would embarrass your father," Adam said with a bit of sternness in his voice.

"I know, my love, and as difficult as it may be I will follow your advice."

They kissed again, and Adam walked to the door and he opened it slightly. They kissed again. He walked down the stairs and into the night.

Twelve

*I*n late March, the St. Lawrence began to thaw and it became obvious the river would be navigable in a few weeks. The men began to collect their equipment to be prepared at a moment's notice. Adam reminded his men that it was a noble cause to meet this Iroquois army, to spread terror among them, and be willing to die for the cause. In the meantime, he encouraged them to make their wills, to take the sacraments of Penitence and Holy Communion, and before the holy alter to pledge themselves by a solemn oath neither to ask for nor to accept any quarter, and to fight to the last breath.

As they knelt for the last time before the alter in the chapel of the Hotel Dieu, that sturdy little population of Ville-Marie gazed upon them with enthusiasm, not unmixed with an envy which had in it nothing ignoble. Some of the chief men of Ville-Marie begged them to wait until the spring sowing was over, that they might join them, but Dollard refused.

The spirit of the enterprise was purely medieval. The enthusiasm of honor, the enthusiasm of adventure, and the enthusiasm of faith were its motivating forces. Dollard was a knight of the early crusades among the forests and savages of the New World. The incidents of this exotic heroism were as definite as a tale of yesterday. The names, ages, and occupations of the seventeen young men may still be read on the ancient register of the parish of Montreal, and the notarial acts of that year, preserved in the records of the city, contain minute accounts of such property as each of them possessed. The three eldest were of twenty-eight, twenty-nine, and thirty-one years, respectively. The age of the rest varied from twenty-one to twenty-seven. They were of various callings: soldiers, armorers, locksmiths, lime-burners, or settlers without trades. The greater number had come to the colony as part of the reinforcement brought by Maisonneuve in 1653.

The time had finally arrived for the mission to begin. After a solemn farewell that included the majority of the residents of Ville-Marie, the governor congratulated them for their bravery and patriotism. Before Adam boarded his canoe, Bernadette put her arms around him and kissed him lightly on the lips. "Goodbye, my brave soldier and future husband," she sternly and tearfully said, "you must come back to me." Adam blushed, kissed her again, turned, and got into his canoe.

So, on the evening of April 15, 1660, the sixteen Frenchmen embarked in several canoes well supplied with arms and ammunition.

Hardly had the canoes left shore when cries were heard coming from the Ile Saint Paul (present day Ile des Soeurs), opposite Ville-Marie. Hastening there, Dollard's troop forced a party of Iroquois to scatter into the woods, but they were too late to save the three Frenchmen who were the victims of this attack: Nicolas Duval had been killed and his companions, Blaise Juillet and Mathurin Soulard, had been drowned while trying to escape from the enemy. Adam seized the Iroquois canoe, took Duval's body back to Ville-Marie, and attended his funeral the next day.

On setting out the second time, the expedition included a seventeenth volunteer who, after failing to keep his word the previous day, had now changed his mind.

Meanwhile, forty warriors of that remnant of the Huron are who, in spite of Iroquois persecutions that still lingered at Quebec, had set out on a war party. They were led by the brave and wily Etienne Annahotaha, their most noted chief. They stopped at Trois Rivieres, where they found a band of Christian Algonquians under a chief named Mituvemeg.

Annahotaha challenged him to a trial of courage, and it was agreed that they should meet at Ville-Marie, where they were likely to find a speedy opportunity of putting their mettle to the test. Accordingly, they departed, the Algonquians with three followers, and the Huron with thirty-nine.

Once they arrived at Ville-Marie, it was not too long before they learned of the departure of Dollard and his companions. This group of friendly Native Americans wished to share the adventure, and to that end the Huron chief asked the governor for a letter to Dollard to serve as credentials. Maisonneuve hesitated. His faith in Huron valor was not great, and he feared the proposed alliance. Nevertheless, he at length yielded so far as to give Annahotaha a letter in which Dollard was told to accept or reject the proffered reinforcement as he should see fit. The Huron's and the Algonquians now embarked and paddled in pursuit of the seventeen Frenchmen.

The rapids above Ville-Marie were swift and challenging. It took them over three days, having to camp during the day in order to go undetected and reach the Lake of Two Mountains. On the fourth day, they reached the mouth of the Ottawa River where it emptied into the Lake.

As they entered the Ottawa, it took another two days to struggle with the strong currents of that river, until finally on the First of May, they reached the foot of the more formidable rapid called the Long Sault. This was where tumult waters, foaming among ledges and boulders, barred the onward way. It was needless to go further. The Iroquois were sure to pass the Sault, and could be fought here as well as elsewhere.

Just below the rapid, where the forest sloped gently to the shore, among a rough clearing stood a palisade fort. This had been the work of an Algonquin war party in the past autumn. It was a mere enclosure of trunks of small trees planted in a circle, and was already in need of repair. They began work immediately to repair this dilapidated structure, felling more trees and building the walls to about ten feet in height. Every few feet, small loopholes were cut in the logs at the height of a man head to allow three men to peer out and point their harquebus at the enemy. They planted a row of stakes within the palisade to form a double fence, and filled the intervening space with earth and stones to the height of a man. One of the French carpenters built a crude door in the structure that would allow ingress and egress to the fort. It was well fortified and could only be opened from the inside.

After several days of physical labor, the Frenchmen took a respite; they made their fires, slung their kettles on the neighboring shore, and settled down for the evening. As the sun set along the reach of the forest, the farther shore basked peacefully in the level rays. The rapids of the river made a tranquil sound that induced a deep sleep to all the Frenchmen who were not standing guard.

The next day, Adam and his band of men scouted the shoreline for the most advantageous places to ambush the Iroquois as they came down the river. Men were placed at these positions in four-hour intervals to ensure that the river was always covered during the daylight hours.

That evening, as Adam and his little army were relaxing and

having an evening meal, the Huron and Algonquin warriors approached, paddling up the Ottawa, and came ashore. Adam recognized this band of Native Americans as being friendly. He remembered being introduced to Annahotaha when he arrived at Quebec.

Annahotaha presented Adam with the letter from the governor of Ville-Marie. Adam was dubious about these allies. He had no experience fighting with them and wondered if they could take orders as he expected from everyone under his command.

Adam invited these new allies to share the evening meal that his men were partaking. Then he turned to Annahotaha and Mituvemeg and requested they follow him back to the little fort. He took them on a short tour of the facility and when it was over, he got down to business. Adam was straight forward in his comments. He reminded them that he was the supreme commander of the operation; they would have to take orders from him and would not be allowed to fight on their own. "Any warrior that does not want to do exactly as I say when the battle begins should leave now," he forcefully said.

Annahotaha and Mituvemeg knew that their warriors could be undisciplined during the heat of a battle. They told Adam that they would speak with their Huron and Algonquin followers and give them an ultimatum: either follow the orders of the French Commander or go back down the river now.

These two Native American chiefs collected their braves and passed on exactly what had been told to them by commander Dollard. They all agreed to the man to follow the orders of Dollard during any ensuing battle.

Adam had Francois Crusson and Rene Dousisin, who were both linguists in Huron and Algonquin languages, to share with these Native Americans the plan for ambushing the Iroquois when they finally came down the river. Dollard further put these two French Militiamen in charge of passing on commands to these native allies once a confrontation with the Iroquois got underway.

Adam had Annahotaha send three Huron and one Algonquin scouts up the river to give advance warning when the Iroquois were about to appear down the Sault.

Midmorning the next day, the Huron scouts came down the river and announced that two Iroquois canoes were coming down the Sault. Adam had time to set his men in ambush among the bushes at a point where he thought the Iroquois were likely to pass.

After about a half hour, it became apparent that he had judged correctly. The canoes carrying five Iroquois came into range and on a given command by Adam, the French and their Indian allies opened fire. Several of the Iroquois were killed or wounded and two escaped into the forest.

Early the next morning, a flotilla of canoes carrying about two hundred Iroquois warriors appeared on the river above. They came bounding down the rapids, filled with warriors eager for revenge.

Adam and his men barely had time to escape to their fort, leaving their kettles still slung over the fires. When the Iroquois landed they made a hasty erratic attack, and were quickly repulsed. Twenty-two Iroquois warriors were either killed or severely wounded during the melee.

A few hours passed while the Iroquois decided what their next step would be. After much talk, they decided to open a parley, hoping, no doubt, to gain some advantage by surprise. When Adam refused to negotiate, the Iroquois began to build a rude fort of their own in the neighboring forest.

These two hundred Iroquois were the advance guard of the main army and were on their way to the Richelieu islands, where six hundred warriors were awaiting them in order to attack the colony in force.

During the next two days, they attacked the little fort where Adam and his men were held up. After the Iroquois were driven back several times with severe losses, the bodies of these warriors began to pile up high against the walls of the fort. On several occasions, a few warriors were able to climb atop their dead comrades and fire directly into the fort, wounding two Huron's and one French fighter. After losing a large number of their warriors, they decided to call to aid the Iroquois army of the Richelieu.

In the meantime, they crouched behind trees and logs, harassing its defenders day and night with a spattering of fire and constant menace of attack. Thus five days passed leaving the occupants of the fort exhausted.

Two canoes of Iroquois paddled with resolve down the Ottawa, into the Lake of Two Mountains and eventually the St. Lawrence. As they passed the little fortress of Ville-Marie, the sentries fired several shots at them. One of the Iroquois was hit in the arm, but continued to paddle in order to get out of range of the forts weapons.

When they finally reached the Richelieu, they had to paddle another five miles to the islands where the Iroquois army was bivouacked. When the word was spread throughout the six hundred warriors, it resulted in a bloodthirsty frenzy. They began to pack immediately. Their chiefs finally took control of this unruly crowd of young warriors, and impressed upon them that taking to the St. Lawrence in the night-time hours would be foolish as well as dangerous. They passed the word that the army would leave for the Ottawa at first light.

As the sun began to shine thought the trees on the little islands of the Richelieu, angry Iroquois warriors launched their canoes and began paddling up the river towards the St. Lawrence. Once the mouth of the Richelieu opened and emptied into the St. Lawrence, the entire flotilla of canoes turned west and continued to paddle with a fury.

Several hours later Ville-Marie came into view. The sentries on the wall of that stockade sounded the alarm. They believed that this Iroquois army was intent on attacking them. The cannon were primed. When the Iroquois flotilla was within firing range, the cannon delivered one of its deadly packages. The Iroquois were paddling so fast that only one of their canoes was hit. The occupants escaped injury and swam to another canoe and were rescued. Before the French on the ramparts could reload the cannon, the Iroquois flotilla was out of range. They rode the rapids above the fort and made their way into the Lake of Two Mountains. After another half day of paddling, these warriors reached the mouth of the Ottawa. They passed with difficulty the swift currents at Carillon and at last the camp of their two hundred brothers came into view.

The excitement of the warriors on the beach at the sight of their reinforcements could be heard within the little fort occupied by the French and their Native American allies. These were not welcome sounds to the besieged. They knew that their chances to survive now were dire.

Thirteen

*A*s the six hundred warriors landed their canoes on the beach, the chiefs went into council. It was noted that many Iroquois had been killed by these stubborn adversaries. The chiefs decided it wasn't worth the sacrifice of more Iroquois deaths, and it would be to their advantage to parlay than to continue to battle. The chiefs deduced that the reason for forming this army was to attack the main settlements of New France. They further deduced that wasting their human resources fighting a few Frenchmen and their Huron and Algonquin allies was futile.

After a few hours, the Iroquois chiefs agreed to have the Seneca chief, Genessee, to open a dialogue with Adam and the Huron chief, Annahotaha. Since the Huron spoke the Iroquoian language, Genessee walked slowly toward the fort, piled high at its front with the dead Iroquois warriors. He found a space between several of his fallen comrades and approached a loophole where he could speak with the leaders within.

Annahotaha and Adam faced him. Genessee addressed his remarks in Iroquoian. Adam depended on Annahotaha to translate. He told them that after a long meeting with all the Iroquois chiefs, they had agreed to allow the occupants of the fort to leave peacefully and return to their respective settlements. After they heard his proposition, they informed Genessee that they needed a few minutes to discuss his proposal. They moved to the other side of the fort where they could speak without being overheard by Genessee.

Annahotaha suggested to Adam that they offer an alternative. Instead of their coming out of their fort, he suggested that the Iroquois army leave instead and paddle down the Ottawa out of sight.

Dollard was sure that they would not accept this suggestion, but what did they have to lose? The number of warriors they were facing now was a formula for their eventual defeat.

Adam and Annahotaha approached the loophole and delivered their counter offer. Genessee stood solemnly and gazed off in the distance. Finally, he turned to Annahotaha and spoke. "If you stay here you will all die?" He took another pause awaiting a reply. When that reply didn't come, he said, "I will take your alternative to my proposal back to the other chiefs, but I am sure what their answer will be." Genessee turned and took about five steps in the direction of the river when one of the Algonquin put his harquebus through a loophole and fired. Genessee fell dead where he stood.

Adam was convinced at this point that the fate of his comrades was sealed. Annahotaha was furious. By killing Genessee, this Algonquin had dishonored an unwritten law of all Native Americans. Annahotaha gave this undisciplined Algonquin a stern reprimand.

No sooner had Annahotaha finished his dressing down of the Algonquin warrior when two Frenchmen charged out of the fort, approached the body of Genessee, and cut off his head. Their countrymen covered them with gunfire while they performed this grisly action. Once the head was removed, the two Frenchmen returned to the fort and placed Genessee's head high on one of the sharpened stakes that overlooked the top of the fort.

The Iroquois, seeing this desecration of the Seneca war chief, howled in a frenzy of helpless rage. They rushed the fort into a barrage of deadly gun fire. One wave of Iroquois after the other were killed or wounded on the spot. Eventually, the warriors in the rear began their attempt to remove their wounded and many of them were killed as well.

The Iroquois were determined, and they rushed up to the pile of corpses only to be turned back again and again. In an act of desperation, they hacked the canoes that were left behind by the occupants of the fort, kindled the bark, and rushed up to pile it blazing against the palisade, but a brisk and steady fire met them that they recoiled and at last gave way. This temporarily dashed their spirits and resolve and they called another council of the chiefs.

In the meantime, the warriors crouched behind trees and logs; they beset the fort, harassing its defenders day and night with a spattering of gun fire and a constant menace of attack.

Another five days passed and things within the fort began to look dire. Although they had ample food, their water supplies began to run low. Annahotaha instructed two of his warriors, under the cover of darkness, to leave the little fort and make their way through the woods and down river of the Iroquois encampment.

At three o'clock in the morning, the two Huron's left the fort and circled around the enclosure and into the woods. In the extreme darkness, they followed their senses and the sounds of the flowing river until after an hour of feeling their way through the thickets stepped onto the beach. They could see the fires burning a few hundred feet away. Unfortunately, they weren't as far away from the Iroquois camp as they would have preferred.

As they were dipping and pouring water from the Ottawa into containers that they had brought along, a war cry surrounded them and in an instant they were approached by a half dozen warriors. They dropped the water containers and ran into the river. The Iroquois went into pursuit.

After a brief struggle, the two Huron's were captured, bound and taken back to the main Iroquois camp. There they were tortured and were each bound to a fallen tree and raised high so they could be observed from the French fort. Dry grass and kindling was piled beneath the two suffering Huron's. At first light, the fuel beneath the bound Huron's was set alight, and they were burned to death in view of the fort.

When the French left Ville-Marie, Adam had several barrels of gunpowder loaded into three canoes and were towed along in back of the flotilla up the Ottawa and stored in their little fort. Adam put his French followers to preparing hand bombs using pieces of rags, gunpowder, and fuses they had brought along as well. Every time the Iroquois would charge the fort they not only faced a heavy barrage of gunfire, but hand bombs thrown into their midst. When one of these bombs would explode, several warriors would be severely burned.

Inside the fort the lack of water became a crisis. Adam ordered one of his engineers to determine where within the fort would be the most advantageous site to dig for an underground water source.

Shortly after the French began digging a well, the Huron warriors confronted Annahotaha that they wanted to parley with the Iroquois. There were several Huron's among the war party that had been adopted into the various Iroquois tribes and they had been calling out to their Huron brothers to defect from the French. Annahotaha used every bit of persuasion he could muster in an attempt to convince them that they couldn't trust the Iroquois to accept them within their ranks. The Iroquois and the Huron's had a long history of fighting a war of extermination.

Years before, a missionary living among the Iroquois asked a Mohawk chief why they were fighting with the Huron's. The missionary couldn't understand why the Iroquois and Huron's couldn't come to some other conclusion to resolve their differences without fighting a war.

"After all, you speak the same language; have all the same customs and religion. There doesn't appear that there are any other differences between you," the missionary inquired.

The Mohawk chief took a long pause as if he was searching for an answer. He looked the missionary in the eye and said, "There are two reasons: first, we don't want to share our hunting grounds with them. But the most important reason is that we are warriors, and that's what warriors do, they fight."

Unfortunately, the little fort was built on a small hill. This made the search for water even more difficult. The French dug down at least ten feet before the soil began to get moist. After two more feet of digging, they finally hit water; however, the well-kept collapsing on itself.

Eventually, Annahotaha couldn't persuade his warriors not to go over to the Iroquois. Adam stepped in and said, "If they want to defect we shouldn't stop them. They are no good to us if they don't have their hearts in this fight."

One of the Huron's put a white shirt on a pole; the gate was open and the forty Huron's moved toward the cheering Iroquois. When the Huron's reached the Iroquois camp they were seized and bound. Five of the Huron's were adopted by Iroquois warriors who had lost their blood brothers in battle. These fortunate Native Americans were allowed to live. In the future, they would recount the battle that had occurred at the Long Sault.

The thirty-four other Huron's were put to a slow death by torture. Annahotaha was the only Huron who didn't defect. He knew that by defecting to the Iroquois would mean a certain death within their fires. His nephew, La Mouche, informed Annahotaha that he too was going to defect. As he was leaving the fort, Annahotaha fired a pistol at him through one of loopholes and killed him instantly.

Three more days wore away in a series of futile attacks made by the Iroquois night and day. During all this time Adam and his men, reeling with exhaustion, fought and prayed as before with vigor.

In the meantime, a detail of men continued to dig deep in the center of the fort in the hope of finding water. Eventually, some water trickled up from the earth, but it was not enough to satisfy their thirst. Adam knew that the lack of water and their meager food supplies, which were becoming exhausted, guaranteed that it was just a matter of time when they would all collapse from thirst and hunger.

He called two of his lieutenants, Jacques Brassier and Robert Jurie, for a conference. He didn't have to explain the dire situation they were in, but he wanted them to know that he was intent on fighting until the end. The end to him was when they were all dead. Surrender was not an option. He called their attention to the two full kegs of gunpowder that was stored within a berm that they had constructed when they first took possession of the little fort.

At that time, there was a lull in the attacks by the Iroquois, but it was just a matter of time when they would launch another assault. Adam instructed his lieutenants to prepare the kegs of gunpowder with fuses and select the strongest man to light a keg and throw it over the top of the palisade when the next attack occurred. He said that he would reserve the second keg for himself. They had their orders and went to work carrying out his commands.

What Adam wasn't aware was that a number of the Iroquois were beginning to leave the battle. Others, however, revolted at the thought that this would be an eternal disgrace to lose so many men at the hands of so paltry an enemy and not to take a full revenge. The remaining chiefs resolved to make a full assault. Volunteers were called for to lead the attack.

As was the custom on such occasions, bundles of small sticks were thrown upon the ground for those who dared picked them up. They would be accepting the challenge to lead the attack.

No precaution was neglected. Large and heavy shields four or five feet high were made by lashing together three split logs with the aid of crossbars. They covered themselves with these mantelets. The chosen band advanced, followed by several hundred warriors. In spite of the brisk fire, they reached the palisade, and, crouching below the range of shot, hewed furiously with their hatchets to cut their way through. The rest followed close and swarmed like angry hornets around the little fort, hacking and tearing to get in.

There were more than one hundred warriors hacking at the front of the palisade. Adam took one of the kegs that had been previously primed with a fuse and lighted it, picked up the keg, and attempted to throw it over the top of the palisade into this throng of angry Iroquois. As he left go of the keg, it struck the ragged top of the palisade and fell back among the Frenchmen within the fort, instantly exploding. It killed and wounded several of them, and nearly blinded all the others.

In the confusion that followed, the Iroquois got possession of the loopholes, and, thrusting in their harquebus, fired on those within. In a moment, they had torn a breach in the palisade, but the French, with energy of desperation, fought like trapped animals.

The Iroquois made another breach and poured into the little fort. Hand-to-hand combat followed. Adam and his followers met the enemy head on. Adam was one of the first to meet his demise when an Iroquois warrior struck him from behind in the head with a hatchet. The other Frenchmen kept up the fight. With a sword or a hatchet in one hand and a knife in the other, they threw themselves against the throng of yelling Iroquois, striking and stabbing with the fury of madmen. The Iroquois, wanting to take them alive, gave in to that attempt and fired at them, volley after volley, until they were all shot down. All was over, and a burst of triumphant yells proclaimed the dear-bought victory.

Searching the pile of corpses, the victors found four Frenchmen still breathing. Three had scarcely a spark of life, and, as no time was to be lost, they burned them on the spot. The fourth, less fortunate, seemed likely to survive, and they reserved him for future torments.

As for the Huron deserters, their cowardice profited them little. The Iroquois, regardless of their promises, fell upon them, burned some at once, and carried the rest to their villages for a similar fate.

Five of the number had the good fortune to escape, and it was from them, aided by admissions made long afterwards by the Iroquois themselves, that the French of New France derived all their knowledge of this glorious disaster.

The heads of the French and Huron dead were removed and impaled on posts around the fort. The Iroquois stayed at the site for another two and a half weeks to bury their dead. The corpses of the French and one Huron were left unburied within the little fort. The Iroquois used the fort for a latrine and the chiefs encouraged the warriors, when using the latrine, to defecate on the remains of their fallen enemy.

To the colony, it proved a salvation. The Iroquois had enough fighting for one season. They had lost about a third of their warriors as a result of the battle. The Iroquois deduced that if seventeen Frenchmen, four Algonquin's, and one Huron, behind a picket fence, could hold eight hundred warriors at bay for so long and kill so many, what might they expect from many more fighting behind walls of stone?

That year they thought no more of capturing Quebec, Ville-Marie, and Trois Rivieres, but went home dejected and amazed, to howl over their losses and nurse their dashed courage for another day of vengeance.

Fourteen

*T*he surviving Frenchman was given to the Mohawk. His name was Rene Doussin who was thirty years old and had been in New France for two years. Little is known of his background and from which area of France he had once lived.

A few weeks after the Mohawk left the Ottawa and paddled down the St. Lawrence and Richelieu rivers, Doussin, hungry and aching, were exultantly displayed to a band of two hundred or so Mohawk braves, who met the returning war party on an island in Lake Champlain. When the canoes landed, the howling warriors danced about in sheer frenzy, slashing at him with their knives and tearing at his flesh with their long fingernails, and then picking up knotty clubs and thorn-studded rods, they formed two parallel lines up the slope of the hill ascending from the beach.

Doussin was forced to run between the columns of club-swinging warriors who delighted in nearly pounding him to death. This was the traditional Mohawk "welcoming committee" for prisoners of war.

With his head bent low, Doussin darted wildly through the mass of swinging cudgels. Blows fell hard and painful on his head, back, neck, and arms, while his sides ached from the sting of the thorny rods being slapped into his flesh and tearing it to pieces. He stumbled to the ground stunned, and they had to drag his unconscious body the rest of the way up the hill.

When he regained his senses, some of his tormentors burned his arms and legs with a torch; others dug their fingernails into his wounds. Someone then took his thumb and crunched it between his teeth with such ferocity that he tore the skin to shreds, exposing the crushed bone.

Doussin was so weak that he could scarcely stand, but it was decided that he was not to be killed. They wanted to triumphantly parade him before the entire Mohawk nation and reserve him for later torments.

With little rest and no food, he was hastened along the trail to the land of the Mohawks. After eighteen days, the agonizing procession at last reached the Mohawk village of Ossernenon. Again, Doussin was subjected to the knives of vicious braves and the nails of seething squaws who sliced and dug at his festering wounds.

The bloodthirsty villagers vied with one another in crunching Doussin's fingers in their mouths, macerating them pitiable, and tearing out the only two fingernails that remained to him. Again the two familiar lines formed and Doussin was forced to run the gauntlet. He had learned how to protect himself from his last experience. He tore through the fray with his head bent low between his arms, but in the end his head was a mass of bloody welts.

They brought out several Algonquian prisoners and marched them to the top of a summit where they were burned and lacerated one by one. Doussin had been tied to a stake. They had one of the Algonquin women prisoners cut off his left thumb with an oyster shell. Some of the remaining Algonquin prisoners and Doussin were taken to a longhouse and stretched out on the ground and bound to stakes. Later that night, little children approached the prisoners and dropped burning coals and fagots on their bare bodies.

Dollard and a few of the Algonquin prisoners were marched to the neighboring village of Andagaron and tortured in much the same manner.

Not long after, a council was held to determine the fate of Doussin and the remaining Algonquin prisoners. The Chiefs decided to spare Doussin and return him to Quebec for a ransom. The Algonquians were put to death.

It was nothing short of a miracle that Doussin recovered from his wounds, but in a few weeks, though scarred and maimed, he was once more on his feet and somewhat stronger. He was allowed to wander the village and fish in the nearby lake. The chiefs informed him that he was to be returned to the French as soon as they could appoint an emissary to accompany him to Quebec. The French were holding a Mohawk Chief they had captured several months before. They were willing to trade Doussin for that chief.

Doussin left three days later, accompanied by a Mohawk chief and four warriors. It was a long and arduous journey, but at last they reached Quebec and were taken directly to the governor. Some of the French at Quebec advised the governor to arrest the Mohawk chief and his escort, but the governor knew that there may be other French prisoners among the Mohawks and not to honor the delegation could endanger future captives. He released the Mohawk Chief, and after entertaining the delegation at his home with a farewell dinner, wished them farewell.

After several weeks of recuperation, Doussin was returned to Ville-Marie and his family. He would never speak about his ordeal as a prisoner of the Mohawks, but he spoke frequently about the bravery of his comrades at the battle at Long Sault. Doussin's was considered the most credible description as to what actually happened at the battle.

EPILOGUE

When the fugitive Huron's reached Ville-Marie, they were unwilling to confess their desertion of the French, and declared that they and some others of their people, to the number of fourteen, had stood by them to the last. This was the story told by one of them to the Jesuit Chaumonot, and by him communicated in a letter to his friends at Quebec. The substance of this letter was given by Marie de l'Incarnation, in her letter to her son of June 25, 1660.

The Jesuit *Relations* of this year gave another long account of the affair, also derived from the Huron deserters, who this time only pretended that ten of their number remained with the French. They afterwards admitted that all had deserted but Annahotaha, as appears from the account drawn up by Dollier de Casson, in his *History of Montreal* and based on Doussin's report.

Belmont, another contemporary, had heard the story from an Iroquois, made the same statement. All these writers, though two of them were not friendly to Ville-Marie, agree that Dollard (Daulac) and his followers saved New France from a disastrous invasion.

The governor, Argenson, in a letter written on the fourth of July following, and in his *Memoire sur le sujet de la guerve des Iroquois*, expressed the same conviction.

Radisson, the famous *voyageur*, said that, on his way down the Ottawa from Lake Superior, he passed the Long Sault a few weeks after the Iroquois had left. He witnessed firsthand the destruction of Dollard and his party, and he gave an account of the fight that answered on the whole to those of the other writers. Based on his observations, the Huron's must have remained outside the fort, since it was too small to hold them. Radisson and his men buried the dead of the fallen defenders within the little fort before continuing their journey to Ville-Marie.

The deaths of Dollard des Ormeaux and his men were recounted by Catholic nuns and entered into official church history. For over a century, Dollard des Ormeaux became a heroic figure in New France, and then in Quebec, who exemplified selfless personal sacrifice, who had been martyrs of the church, and for the colony. Historians in the19th century converted the battle into a religious and nationalistic epic in which zealous Roman Catholics deliberately sacrificed themselves to fend off an attack on New France.

However, there were other versions of the story, even then, that raised questions about Dollard's intentions and actions. For one, many historians now believe that Dollard and his men went up the Ottawa River for other reasons and did not even know of the approaching Iroquois. Nevertheless, Dollard did indeed divert the Iroquois army temporarily from its objective in 1660, thereby allowing the settlers to harvest their crop and escape famine.

Some historians have claimed that all Frenchmen including Dollard were killed in the last valiant explosion of the famous grenade that had not made it over the wall of the fort and landed in the midst of the remaining French. Others claim that some were captured and tortured to death, and some extreme cases were even cannibalized by the Iroquois. Also there are variations as to who delivered the grim news to the French at Ville-Marie; others claim that the Catholic nuns recounted the story.

Modern historians have looked beyond the politically charged elements surrounding Dollard des Ormeaux and have come up with theories that differ from the traditionally told stories of his life and demise. For instance, some have hypothesized that Dollard's motivation for heading west from Ville-Marie may not have been to head off the Iroquois war party. Instead, it was well known at the time that the Iroquois finished their hunting expeditions for furs in the spring, and an enterprising Frenchman with military experience, such as Dollard, may have been tempted to test his mettle by risking the voyage up the Ottawa River.

Still some historians have also posited that the Iroquois did not continue to Ville-Marie because it was not representative of Iroquois warfare tactics. Iroquois war parties sought the trophies of battle and taking prisoners. If Dollard des Ormeaux and his party did indeed stave off the Iroquois attack for several days, their defeat would have satisfied that goal and aspect of Iroquoian warfare.

The location of the battle is a topic of intense controversy. Traditionally, the battle was fought along the Ottawa River near Carrillon, Quebec. This location is based on nationalistic traditions on the part of Quebec historians. Supporters of this location also refer to the countless texts written after the event and for many years after maintain this tradition.

However, other scholars place the event on the northern side of the Ottawa River on the now Ross Farm in Ontario. The location being neither in Ontario or Quebec has cultural implications. However, both sides of the debate agree that Dollard and his both French and Indigenous comrades would have taken the route following the Ottawa River since they sought to intercept the Iroquois coming back from their winter hunt. Similar to the Carillon advocates, the Ross Farm advocates, in part, base their conclusions on tradition.

Traditions include known battles between French and Iroquois in this area, old French inhabitants of the area placing the battle there, and also from testimony of a Huron eyewitness to the battle.

Archeological evidence is also referenced by Ross Farm advocates. Archeological excavations of palisades (in which Dollard and his comrades fought within) and considerations of topography coincide with the testimonies of the Huron survivors along with other oral and written traditions.

The first sources written concerning the Battle of Long Sault are a series of letters composed by Marie Guyart, founder of the Ursuline institute of New France, and a collection of compiled documents from various Jesuit missionaries entitled *Relations*. These sources, written immediately after Dollard's death in 1660, give descriptive accounts of the battle and emphasize the dualism between Christianity and barbarism of the Native Americans.

Although he is singled out as the leader in these earliest recorded stories, Dollard des Ormeaux is not the main focus of the battle.

In 1672, Francois Dollier de Casson wrote *Histoire de Montreal*. His book included a chapter dedicated solely to Dollard des Ormeaux and the Battle of Long Sault. This work marked a shift in Dollard's personal role in the battle. In Dollier's account, Dollard becomes a central heroic figure. He is characterized by an air of mystery and strong leadership abilities. He also occupies a more active role in the proceedings. Similar to Guyart's account, Dollard is aligned with Christianity in opposition to the barbarism of the Natives.

These accounts of Dollard provide a basis that allowed him to develop into and be upheld as a heroic figure in French-Canadian culture, post-British conquest. These sources also set a precedent of anti-Native American sentiment surrounding the veneration of Dollard.

With the exception of a brief mention in the work of Charlevoix in the 1700s, Dollard and the Battle of Long Sault does not reappear in French Canadian writing until the 1840s. The re-emergence of the tale coincides with the union of Upper and Lower Canada and the ensuing fear that French Canadians would lose control over their rights. The Story of Dollard was used by authors in this period, such as Francois-Xavier Garneau, to secure a space for the French in the national history of Canada. Garneau's text emphasizes the loyalty of Dollard and his soldiers to their nation and the unity of their action.

The rise of industrialization and ultamontanism in the 1860s marked another shift in the story of Dollard. The Catholic Church had become an influential representative of French Canadian interests within the country.

In 1865, Etienne-Michel Faillon published L'Histoire de la colonie francaise au Canada which included an account of the Battle of Long Sault. Faillon's writing places heavy emphasis on the duality between Christianity and barbarity. The language used by Faillon is aggrandizing and glorifies Dollard and his soldier's far more than previous accounts. Dollard, in Faillon's account, becomes an ideal model of Christian morality. Faillon's text became the canon of the Dollard story in French Canadian culture.

This attitude was perpetuated throughout the early 1900s. The writing of Lionel Groulx's writing, in particular, emphasizes the youth of Dollard and upholds him as a model for French Canadian children.

Since controversy has come to light surrounding the circumstances of the Battle of Long Sault, modern historians have challenged traditional visions of Dollard as a hero in Quebec culture.

There have been tributes to Dollard des Ormeaux in Canadian poetry, theater, and literature. As a response to French marginalization throughout Canada, a lot of this work generally focuses on themes of heroism and the strength of French Canadian ancestors. The art also often explores Dollard's martyrdom for the growth of the nation. The Native Americans are largely absent in these bodies of work and when represented; often they are depicted as negative figures.

A monument to Dollard des Ormeaux, created by sculptor Alfred Laliberte and the architect Alphonse Venne, was inaugurated in Parc Lafontaine on June 24, 1920.

A bas-relief on the Maisonneuve Monument at Place d'Armes, Montreal, sculpted by Louis-Philippe Hebert, portrays Dollard des Ormeaux in the Battle of Long Sault.

In Quebec, starting during the time of the Quiet Revolution, Victoria Day became unofficially known as Fete de Dollard. In 2003, provincial legislation officially declared the date to be National Patriots' Day.

Finally, although as previously mentioned, some historians have posited that the Iroquois did not continue to Ville-Marie because it was not representative of Iroquois warfare tactics. Iroquois war parties sought the trophies of battle and taking prisoners. Therefore, it is believed that if Dollard des Ormeaux and his party did indeed stave off the Iroquois attack for several days, their defeat would have satisfied that goal and aspect of

Iroquoian warfare.

Of course many other historians disagree with that proposition. They believe that the Iroquois were soundly demoralized by losing a third of their army by a few French, and for a while a few Native Americans, and had lost their will to continue their assault against the New French colonies.

I agree with the latter proposition.

Lee Dorsey, Author

As a side note: Bernadette Maisonneuve, after it was learned that Adam Dollard died fighting at the Long Sault, moved to Quebec and taught school with the nuns to the colonists and Algonquin children. In 1572, she contacted pneumonia and after several weeks of suffering, died. It should be pointed out that in all that time, she never married.

About the Author

Lee Dorsey attended the American University in Washington, D.C., and holds a Master's Degree in Human Resources Management. He worked in broadcasting for several years, and after which, he worked for the United States Naval Academy, where he was eventually promoted to Director of Human Resources for the Brigade Services Division. He retired from the USNA in 2008 and began a new career as a writer.

He currently writes fulltime, and is the author of several published novels, including *A Forbidden Love, Mercenaries of Panama, I and II, Indiscretions, The Artist, Androgyny, A Search for Love, The Triangulum Galaxy and Whatever Happened to Virginia Dare.*